THIS REMARKABLE VOLUME
OF SCIENCE FICTION

is an attempt to answer what might be called "the Kornbluth problem"—a question which usually has two aspects:

What makes Kornbluth so much fun to read?

AND

Where can I find more?

As for the delights of Kornbluth, there are many theories —his uncanny precision with language, for example, or his deftly ironic sense of the consequences of ideas.

But perhaps the most satisfying way of settling both questions is simply to read further. For here—in such brilliant stories as "The Mindworm," "Gomez," and "The Rocket of 1955"—he is at his brilliant best. And here, in this far-ranging collection, the demand for a comprehensive selection of the truly unusual work of C. M. Kornbluth has at last been met.

(Except for this Note, this edition of THE EXPLORERS appears as it was first published in 1954, before C. M. Kornbluth's death.)

by C. M. Kornbluth

TAKEOFF
THE SYNDIC
THE EXPLORERS

with Frederik Pohl

THE SPACE MERCHANTS
SEARCH THE SKY

THIS IS AN ORIGINAL COLLECTION—NOT A REPRINT—
PUBLISHED BY BALLANTINE BOOKS, INC.

The Explorers

SHORT STORIES

by C. M. KORNBLUTH

BALLANTINE BOOKS   •   NEW YORK

Printing History:

First edition: August, 1954
Second edition: March, 1963

BALLANTINE BOOKS, INC.
101 FIFTH AVENUE, NEW YORK 3, N. Y.

To my parents,

Samuel and Deborah Kornbluth

Foreword

BY FREDERIK POHL

IN THE beginning there was S. D. Gottesman. Gottesman was born in the early stages of World War II, and science-fiction readers liked him very much. He became a fixture in half-a-dozen magazines of the time—some of them no longer with us—and shortly was joined by a number of other by-lines, attached to much the same sort of wry and colorful story. There was Cecil Corwin and Ganriel Barclay and Walter C. Davies and a good many more, and if the stories seemed closely related to each other, it was easy enough to understand. For behind these pen-names—eighteen or nineteen of them—stood a single bland-faced, sharp-tongued teen-ager, whose real name was Cyril Kornbluth.

How many stories did Kornbluth write before he was old enough to vote? Legend says dozens—but legend is wrong, for in truth the number was in the scores. There were magazines which, for the *total* length of their careers, published more words originally set on paper by Kornbluth than by all their other contributors combined. But all of the stories were masked; it was not until after the war that Kornbluth's own name first appeared in a magazine . . . and, at that, the magazines were detective stories, not science fiction.

But then Kornbluth came back to the fold. Casting the pseudonymous chrysalids off, he settled down to serious work. He began writing wonderful little short stories—like "The Mindworm" and "Friend to Man." That was easy enough, so he raised his sights to novelettes; and the extra length allowed him extra scope to delve into the whole complex structure of the future societies he envisioned. "That Share of Glory" is an example—a detailed and plausible and, once you look at it closely, a frighteningly clear look into Kornbluth's private crystal ball. By then he had hit his stride; and the results have delighted hundreds of thousands of readers. Novels—brilliant ones—like THE SYNDIC and TAKEOFF; short stories and novelettes besides.

It is probably untrue that science-fiction magazines would have suspended publication if there had been no Kornbluth—but they would not have been nearly as much fun. Kornbluth is a very special favorite of my own—as anyone might come to suspect from the fact that he and I have collaborated on many stories together, shorts and novelettes in the old days, more recently such novels as THE SPACE MERCHANTS, SEARCH THE SKY, and GLADIATOR-AT-LAW. But it is no personal prejudice, I vow, that makes me say that Kornbluth the Writer is something worth watching. For brilliant conceptions and literate use of words, for exciting imagination and characters to make it real, the science-fiction field is fortunate in many talented writers—but none better than he.

—*Frederik Pohl*

Contents

Gomez

NOW that I'm a cranky, constipated old man I can afford to say that the younger generation of scientists makes me sick to my stomach. Short order fry-cooks of destruction, they hear through the little window the dim order: "Atom bomb rare, with cobalt 60!" and sing it back and rattle their stinking skillets and sling the deadly hash—just what the customer ordered, with never a notion invading their smug, too-heated havens that there's a small matter of right and wrong that takes precedence even over their haute cuisine.

There used to be a slew of them who yelled to high heaven about it. Weiner, Urey, Szilard, Morrison—dead now, and worse. Unfashionable. The greatest of them you have never heard of. Admiral MacDonald never did clear the story. He was Julio Gomez, and his story was cleared yesterday by a fellow my Jewish friends call Malach Hamovis, the Hovering Angel of Death. A black-bordered letter from Rosa advised me that Malach Hamovis had come in on runway six with his flaps down and picked up Julio at the age of 39. Pneumonia.

"But," Rosa painfully wrote, "Julio would want you to know he died not too unhappy, after a good though short life with much of satisfaction . . ."

I think it will give him some more satisfaction, wherever he is, to know that his story at last is getting told.

It started twenty-two years ago with a routine assignment on a crisp October morning. I had an appointment with Dr. Sugarman, the head of the physics department at the University. It was the umpth anniversary of something or other—

1

first atomic pile, the test A-bomb, Nagasaki—I don't remember what, and the Sunday editor was putting together a page on it. My job was to interview the three or four University people who were Manhattan District grads.

I found Sugarman in his office at the top of the modest physics building's square gothic tower, brooding through a pointed-arch window at the bright autumn sky. He was a tubby, jowly little fellow. I'd been seeing him around for a couple of years at testimonial banquets and press conferences, but I didn't expect him to remember me. He did, though, and even got the name right.

"Mr. Vilchek?" he beamed. "From the *Tribune*?"

"That's right, Dr. Sugarman. How are you?"

"Fine; fine. Sit down, please. Well, what shall we talk about?"

"Well, Dr. Sugarman, I'd like to have your ideas on the really fundamental issues of atomic energy, A-bomb control and so on. What in your opinion is the single most important factor in these problems?"

His eyes twinkled; he was going to surprise me. "Education!" he said, and leaned back waiting for me to register shock.

I registered. "That's certainly a different approach, doctor. How do you mean that, exactly?"

He said impressively: "Education—*technical* education—is the key to the underlying issues of our time. I am deeply concerned over the unawareness of the general public to the meaning and accomplishments of science. People underrate me—underrate *science*, that is—because they do not *understand* science. Let me show you something." He rummaged for a moment through papers on his desk and handed me a sheet of lined tablet paper covered with chicken-track handwriting. "A letter I got," he said. I squinted at the penciled scrawl and read:

October 12

Esteemed Sir:
    Beg to introduce self to you the atomic Scientist as a youth 17 working with diligence to perfect self in Mathematical Physics. The knowledge of English is imperfect since am in New-York 1 year only from Puerto Rico and due to Father and Mother poverty

*must wash the dishes in the restaurant. So esteemed
sir excuse imperfect English which will better.*

*I hesitate intruding your valuable Scientist time
but hope you sometime spare minutes for diligents
such as I. My difficulty is with neutron cross-section
absorption of boron steel in Reactor which theory I
am working out. Breeder reactors demand*

$$u = \frac{x}{1} + \frac{x^5}{1} + \frac{x^{10}}{1} + \frac{x^{15}}{1} + \cdots$$

*for boron steel, compared with neutron cross-section
absorption of*

$$v = \frac{x^{1/5}}{1} + \frac{x}{1} + \frac{x^2}{1} + \frac{x^3}{1} + \cdots$$

*for any Concrete with which I familiarize myself.
Whence arises relationship*

$$v^5 = u \; \frac{1 - 2u + 4u^3 - 3u^2 + u^4}{1 + 3u + 4u^2 + 2u^3 + u^4}$$

*indicating only a fourfold breeder gain. Intuitively I
dissatisfy with this gain and beg to intrude your time
to ask wherein I neglect. With the most sincere
thanks.*

J. Gomez
% Porto Bello Lunchroom
124th St. & St. Nicholas Ave.
New-York, New-York

I laughed and told Dr. Sugarman appreciatively: "That's a
good one. I wish our cranks kept in touch with us by mail, but
they don't. In the newspaper business they come in and demand to see the editor. Could I use it, by the way? The readers
ought to get a boot out of it."

He hesitated and said: "All right—if you don't use my
name. Just say 'a prominent physicist.' I didn't think it was
too funny myself though, but I see your point, of course. The
boy may be feeble-minded—and he probably is—but he be-
lieves, like too many people, that science is just a bag of
tricks which any ordinary person can acquire—"

And so on and so on.

I went back to the office and wrote the interview in twenty

minutes. It took me longer than that to talk the Sunday editor into running the Gomez letter in a box on the atom-anniversary page, but he finally saw it my way. I had to retype it. If I'd just sent the letter down to the composing room as was, we would have had a strike on our hands.

On Sunday morning, at a quarter past six, I woke up to the tune of fists thundering on my hotel-room door. I found my slippers and bathrobe and lurched blearily across the room. They didn't wait for me to unlatch. The door opened. I saw one of the hotel clerks, the Sunday editor, a frosty-faced old man and three hard-faced, hard-eyed young men. The hotel clerk mumbled and retreated and the others moved in. "Chief," I asked the Sunday editor hazily, "what's going—?"

A hard-faced young man was standing with his back to the door; another was standing with his back to the window and the third was blocking the bathroom door. The icy old man interrupted me with a crisp authoritative question snapped at the editor. "You identify this man as Vilchek?"

The editor nodded.

"Search him," snapped the old man. The fellow standing guard at the window slipped up and frisked me for weapons while I sputtered incoherently and the Sunday editor avoided my eye.

When the search was over the frosty-faced old boy said to me: "I am Rear Admiral MacDonald, Mr. Vilchek. I'm here in my capacity as deputy director of the Office of Security and Intelligence, U. S. Atomic Energy Commission. Did you write this?" He thrust a newspaper clipping at my face.

I read, blearily:

WHAT'S SO TOUGH ABOUT A-SCIENCE?
TEENAGE POT-WASHER DOESN'T KNOW

A letter received recently by a prominent local atomic scientist points up Dr. Sugarman's complaint (see adjoining column) that the public does not appreciate how hard a physicist works. The text, complete with "mathematics" follows:

Esteemed Sir:

Beg to introduce self to you the Atomic Scientist as youth 17 working——

"Yes," I told the admiral. "I wrote it, except for the head-line. What about it?"

He snapped: "The letter is purportedly from a New York youth seeking information, yet there is no address for him given. Why is that?"

I said patiently: "I left it off when I copied it for the composing room. That's *Trib* style on readers' letters. *What* is all this about?"

He ignored the question and asked: "Where is the purported original of the letter?"

I thought hard and told him: "I think I stuck it in my pants pocket. I'll get it—" I started for the chair with my suit draped over it.

"Hold it, mister!" said the young man at the bathroom door. I held it and he proceeded to go through the pockets of the suit. He found the Gomez letter in the inside breast pocket of the coat and passed it to the admiral. The old man compared it, word for word, with the clipping and then put them both in his pocket.

"I want to thank you for your cooperation," he said coldly to me and the Sunday editor. "I caution you not to discuss, and above all not to publish, any account of this incident. The national security is involved in the highest degree. Good day."

He and his boys started for the door, and the Sunday editor came to life. "Admiral," he said, "this is going to be on the front page of tomorrow's *Trib*."

The admiral went white. After a long pause he said: "You are aware that this country may be plunged into global war at any moment. That American boys are dying every day in border skirmishes. Is it to protect civilians like you who won't obey a reasonable request affecting security?"

The Sunday editor took a seat on the edge of my rumpled bed and lit a cigarette. "I know all that, admiral," he said. "I also know that this is a free country and how to keep it that way. Pitiless light on incidents like this of illegal search and seizure."

The admiral said: "I personally assure you, on my honor as an officer, that you would be doing the country a grave disservice by publishing an account of this."

The Sunday editor said mildly: "Your honor as an officer. You broke into this room without a search warrant. Don't you realize that's against the law? And I saw your boy ready to shoot when Vilchek started for that chair." I began to sweat a little at that, but the admiral was sweating harder.

With an effort he said: "I should apologize for the abruptness and discourtesy with which I've treated you. I do apologize. My only excuse is that, as I've said, this is a crash-priority matter. May I have your assurance that you gentlemen will keep silent?"

"On one condition," said the Sunday editor. "I want the *Trib* to have an exclusive on the Gomez story. I want Mr. Vilchek to cover it, with your full cooperation. In return, we'll hold it for your release and submit it to your security censorship."

"It's a deal," said the admiral, sourly. He seemed to realize suddenly that the Sunday editor had been figuring on such a deal all along.

On the plane for New York, the admiral filled me in. He was precise and unhappy, determined to make the best of a bad job. "I was awakened at three this morning by a phone call from the chairman of the Atomic Energy Commission. *He* had been awakened by a call from Dr. Monroe of the Scientific Advisory Committee. Dr. Monroe had been up late working and sent out for the Sunday *Tribune* to read before going to sleep. He saw the Gomez letter and went off like a 16-inch rifle. The neutron cross-section absorption relationship expressed in it happens to be, Mr. Vilchek, his own work. It also happens to be one of the nation's most closely-guarded—er—atomic secrets. Presumably this Gomez stumbled on it somehow, as a janitor or something of the sort, and is feeding his ego by pretending to be an atomic scientist."

I scratched my unshaved jaw. "Admiral," I said, "you wouldn't kid me? How can three equations be a top atomic secret?"

The admiral hesitated. "All I can tell you," he said slowly, "is that breeder reactors are involved."

"But the letter said that. You mean this Gomez not only swiped the equations but knew what they were about?"

The admiral said grimly: "Somebody has been incredibly lax. It would be worth many divisions to the Soviet for their man Kapitza to see those equations—and realize that they are valid."

He left me to chew that one over for a while as the plane droned over New Jersey. Finally the pilot called back: "E.T.A. five minutes, sir. We have landing priority at Newark."

"Good," said the admiral. "Signal for a civilian-type car to pick us up without loss of time."

"Civilian," I said.

"Of course civilian!" he snapped. "That's the hell of it. Above all we must not arouse suspicion that there is anything special or unusual about this Gomez or his letter. Copies of the *Tribune* are on their way to the Soviet now as a matter of routine—they take all American papers and magazines they can get. If we tried to stop shipment of *Tribunes* that would be an immediate give-away that there was something of importance going on."

We landed and the five of us got into a late-model car, neither drab nor flashy. One of the admiral's young men relieved the driver, a corporal with Signal Corps insignia. There wasn't much talk during the drive from Newark to Spanish Harlem, New York. Just once the admiral lit a cigarette, but he flicked it through the window after a couple of nervous puffs.

The Porto Bello Lunchroom was a store-front restaurant in the middle of a shabby tenement block. Wide-eyed, graceful, skinny little kids stared as our car parked in front of it and then converged on us purposefully. "Watch your car, mister?" they begged. The admiral surprised them—and me—with a flood of Spanish that sent the little extortionists scattering back to their stickball game in the street and their potsy layouts chalked on the sidewalks.

"Higgins," said the admiral, "see if there's a back exit." One of his boys got out and walked around the block under the dull, incurious eyes of black-shawled women sitting on their stoops. He was back in five minutes, shaking his head.

"Vilchek and I will go in," said the admiral. "Higgins, stand by the restaurant door and tackle anyone who comes flying out. Let's go, reporter. And remember that I do the talking."

The noon-hour crowd at the Porto Bello's ten tables looked up at us when we came in. The admiral said to a woman at a primitive cashier's table: "*Nueva York* Board of Health, *señora.*"

"Ah!" she muttered angrily. *"Por favor, no aquí!* In back, understand? Come." She beckoned a pretty waitress to take over at the cash drawer and led us into the steamy little kitchen. It was crowded with us, an old cook and a young dishwasher. The admiral and the woman began a rapid exchange of Spanish. He played his part well. I myself couldn't keep my eyes off the kid dishwasher who somehow or other had got hold of one of America's top atomic secrets.

Gomez was seventeen, but he looked fifteen. He was small-boned and lean, with skin the color of bright Virginia tobacco in an English cigarette. His hair was straight and glossy-black and a little long. Every so often he wiped his hands on his apron and brushed it back from his damp forehead. He was working like hell, dipping and swabbing and rinsing and drying like a machine, but he didn't look pushed or angry. He wore a half-smile that I later found out was his normal, relaxed expression and his eyes were far away from the kitchen of the Porto Bello Lunchroom. The elderly cook was making it clear by the exaggerated violence of his gesture and a savage frown that he resented these people invading his territory. I don't think Gomez even knew we were there. A sudden, crazy idea came into my head.

The admiral had turned to him. *"Como se llama, chico?"*

He started and put down the dish he was wiping. "Julio Gomez, *señor. Por que, por favor? Que pasa?"*

He wasn't the least bit scared.

"Nueva York Board of Health," said the admiral. *"Con su permiso—"* He took Gomez' hands in his and looked at them gravely, front and back, making *tsk-tsk* noises. Then, decisively: *"Vamanos, Julio. Siento mucho. Usted esta muy enfermo."* Everybody started talking at once, the woman doubtless objecting to the slur on her restaurant and the cook to losing his dishwasher and Gomez to losing time from the job.

The admiral gave them broadside for broadside and outlasted them. In five minutes we were leading Gomez silently from the restaurant. *"La lotería!"* a woman customer said in a loud whisper. *"O las mutas,"* somebody said back. Arrested for policy or marihuana, they thought. The pretty waitress at the cashier's table looked stricken and said nervously: "Julio?" as we passed, but he didn't notice.

Gomez sat in the car with the half-smile on his lips and his eyes a million miles away as we rolled downtown to Foley Square. The admiral didn't look as though he'd approve of any questions from me. We got out at the Federal Building and Gomez spoke at last. He said in surprise: "This, it is not the hospital!"

Nobody answered. We marched him up the steps and surrounded him in the elevator. It would have made anybody nervous—it would have made *me* nervous—to be herded like that; everybody's got something on his conscience. But the kid didn't even seem to notice. I decided that he must be a half-wit or—there came that crazy notion again.

The glass door said "U. S. Atomic Energy Commission, Office of Security and Intelligence." The people behind it were flabbergasted when the admiral and party walked in. He turned the head man out of his office and sat at his desk, with Gomez getting the caller's chair. The rest of us stationed ourselves uncomfortably around the room.

It started. The admiral produced the letter and asked in English: "Have you ever seen this before?" He made it clear from the way he held it that Gomez wasn't going to get his hands on it.

"*Si, seguro.* I write it last week. This is funny business. I am not really sick like you say, no?" He seemed relieved.

"No. Where did you get these equations?"

Gomez said proudly: "I work them out."

The admiral gave a disgusted little laugh. "Don't waste my time, boy. Where did you get these equations?"

Gomez was beginning to get upset. "You got no right to call me liar," he said. "I not so smart as the big physicists, *seguro*, and maybe I make mistakes. Maybe I waste the *profesór* Soo-har-man his time but he got no right to have me arrest. I tell him right in letter he don't have to answer if he don't want. I make no crime and you got no right!"

The admiral looked bored. "Tell me how you worked the equations out," he said.

"Okay," said Gomez sulkily. "You know the random paths of neutron is expressed in matrix mechanics by *profesór* Oppenheim five years ago, all okay. I transform his equations from path-prediction domain to cross-section domain and integrate over absorption areas. This gives u series and v series. And from there, the u-v relationship is obvious, no?"

The admiral, still bored, asked: "Got it?"

I noticed that one of his young men had a shorthand pad out. He said: "Yes."

The admiral picked up the phone and said: "This is Mac-Donald. Get me Dr. Mines out at Brookhaven right away." He told Gomez blandly: "Dr. Mines is the chief of the A.E.C. Theoretical Physics Division. I'm going to ask him what he thinks of the way you worked the equations out. He's going to tell me that you were just spouting a lot of gibberish. And then you're going to tell me where you *really* got them."

Gomez looked mixed up and the admiral turned back to the phone. "Dr. Mines? This is Admiral MacDonald of Security. I want your opinion on the following." He snapped his fingers impatiently and the stenographer passed him his pad. "Somebody has told me that he discovered a certain relationship by taking—" He read carefully. "—by taking the random paths of a neutron expressed in matrix mechanics by Oppenheim, transforming his equations from the path-prediction domain to the cross-section domain and integrating over the absorption areas."

In the silence of the room I could hear the faint buzz of the voice on the other end. And a great red blush spread over the admiral's face from his brow to his neck. The faintly-buzzing voice ceased and after a long pause the admiral said slowly and softly: "No, it wasn't Fermi or Szilard. I'm not at liberty to tell you who. Can you come right down to the Federal Building Security Office in New York? I—I need your help. Crash priority." He hung up the phone wearily and muttered to himself: "Crash priority. Crash." And wandered out of the office looking dazed.

His young men stared at one another in frank astonishment. "Five years," said one, "and—"

"*Nix*," said another, looking pointedly at me.

Gomez asked brightly: "What goes on anyhow? This is damn funny business, I think."

"Relax, kid," I told him. "Looks as if you'll make out all—"

"*Nix*," said the nixer again savagely, and I shut up and waited.

After a while somebody came in with coffee and sandwiches and we ate them. After another while the admiral came in with Dr. Mines. Mines was a white-haired, wrinkled Connecticut Yankee. All I knew about him was that he'd been in mild trouble with Congress for stubbornly plugging world government and getting on some of the wrong letterheads. But I learned right away that he was all scientist and didn't have a phony bone in his body.

"Mr. Gomez?" he asked cheerfully. "The admiral tells me that you are either a well-trained Russian spy or a phenomenal self-taught nuclear physicist. He wants me to find out which."

"Russia?" yelled Gomez, outraged. "He crazy! I am American United States citizen!"

"That's as may be," said Dr. Mines. "Now, the admiral tells me you describe the *u-v* relationship as 'obvious.' I should call it a highly abstruse derivation in the theory of continued fractions and complex multiplication."

Gomez strangled and gargled helplessly trying to talk, and finally asked, his eyes shining: *"Por favor,* could I have piece paper?"

They got him a stack of paper and the party was on.

For two unbroken hours Gomez and Dr. Mines chattered and scribbled. Mines gradually shed his jacket, vest and tie, completely oblivious to the rest of us. Gomez was even more abstracted. He *didn't* shed his jacket, vest and tie. He didn't seem to be aware of anything except the rapid-fire exchange of ideas via scribbled formulae and the terse spoken jargon of mathematics. Dr. Mines shifted on his chair and sometimes his voice rose with excitement. Gomez didn't shift or wriggle or cross his legs. He just sat and scribbled and talked in a low, rapid monotone, looking straight at Dr. Mines with his eyes very wide-open and lit up like searchlights.

The rest of us just watched and wondered.

Dr. Mines broke at last. He stood up and said: "I can't take any more, Gomez. I've got to think it over—" He began to leave the room, mechanically scooping up his clothes, and then realized that we were still there.

"Well?" asked the admiral grimly.

Dr. Mines smiled apologetically. "He's a physicist, all right," he said. Gomez sat up abruptly and looked astonished.

"Take him into the next office, Higgins," said the admiral. Gomez let himself be led away, like a sleepwalker.

Dr. Mines began to chuckle. "Security!" he said. "Security!"

The admiral rasped: "Don't trouble yourself over my decisions, if you please, Dr. Mines. My job is keeping the Soviets from pirating American science and I'm doing it to the best of my ability. What I want from you is your opinion on the possibility of that young man having worked out the equations as he claimed."

Dr. Mines was abruptly sobered. "Yes," he said. "Unquestionably he did. And will you excuse my remark? I was under some strain in trying to keep up with Gomez."

"Certainly," said the admiral, and managed a frosty smile. "Now if you'll be so good as to tell me how this completely impossible thing can have happened—?"

"It's happened before, admiral," said Dr. Mines. "I don't suppose you ever heard of Ramanujan?"

"No."

"*Srinivasa* Ramanujan?"

"*No!*"

"Oh. Well, Ramanujan was born in 1887 and died in 1920. He was a poor Hindu who failed twice in college and then settled down as a government clerk. With only a single obsolete textbook to go on he made himself a very great mathematician. In 1913 he sent some of his original work to a Cambridge professor. He was immediately recognized and called to England where he was accepted as a first-rank man, became a member of the Royal Society, a Fellow of Trinity and so forth."

The admiral shook his head dazedly.

"It happens," Dr. Mines said. "Oh yes, it happens. Ramanujan had only one out-of-date book. But this is New York. Gomez has access to all the mathematics he could hope for and a great mass of unclassified and declassified nuclear data. And—genius. The way he puts things together . . . he seems to have only the vaguest notion of what a proof should be. He *sees* relationships as a whole. A most convenient faculty which I envy him. Where I have to take, say, a dozen painful steps from one conclusion to the next he achieves it in one grand flying leap. Ramanujan was like that too, by the way— very strong on intuition, weak on what we call 'rigor.'" Dr. Mines noted with a start that he was holding his tie, vest and coat in one hand and began to put them on. "Was there anything else?" he asked politely.

"One thing," said the admiral. "Would you say he's—he's a better physicist than you are?"

"Yes," said Dr. Mines. "Much better." And he left.

The admiral slumped, uncharacteristically, at the desk for a long time. Finally he said to the air: "Somebody get me the

General Manager. No, the Chairman of the Commission."
One of his boys grabbed the phone and got to work on the
call.

"Admiral," I said, "where do we stand now?"

"Eh? Oh, it's you. The matter's out of my hands now since
no security violation is involved. I consider Gomez to be in
my custody and I shall turn him over to the Commission so
that he may be put to the best use in the nation's interest."

"Like a machine?" I asked, disgusted.

He gave me both barrels of his ice-blue eyes. "Like a
weapon," he said evenly.

He was right, of course. Didn't I know there was a war on?
Of course I did. Who didn't? Taxes, housing shortage, somebody's cousin killed in Korea, everybody's kid brother sweating out the draft, prices sky-high at the supermarket.
Uncomfortably I scratched my unshaved chin and walked to
the window. Foley Square below was full of Sunday peace,
with only a single girl stroller to be seen. She walked the length
of the block across the street from the Federal Building and
then turned and walked back. Her walk was dragging and
hopeless and tragic.

Suddenly I knew her. She was the pretty little waitress from
the Porto Bello; she must have hopped a cab and followed
the men who were taking her Julio away. Might as well beat
it, sister, I told her silently. Julio isn't just a good-looking kid
any more; he's a military asset. The Security Office is turning
him over to the policy-level boys for disposal. When that
happens you might as well give up and go home.

It was as if she'd heard me. Holding a silly little handkerchief to her face she turned and ran blindly for the subway
entrance at the end of the block and disappeared into it.

At that moment the telephone rang.

"MacDonald here," said the admiral. "I'm ready to report
on the Gomez affair, Mr. Commissioner."

Gomez was a minor, so his parents signed a contract for
him. The job-description on the contract doesn't matter, but
he got a pretty good salary by government standards and a
per-diem allowance too.

I signed a contract, too—"Information Specialist." I was
partly companion, partly historian and partly a guy they'd
rather have their eyes on than not. When somebody tried to

cut me out on grounds of economy, Admiral MacDonald frostily reminded him that he had given his word. I stayed, for all the good it did me.

We didn't have any name. We weren't Operation Anything or Project Whoozis or Task Force Dinwiddie. We were just five people in a big fifteen-room house on the outskirts of Milford, New Jersey. There was Gomez, alone on the top floor with a lot of books, technical magazines and blackboards and a weekly visit from Dr. Mines. There were the three Security men, Higgins, Dalhousie and Leitzer, sleeping by turns and prowling the grounds. And there was me.

From briefing sessions with Dr. Mines I kept a diary of what went on. Don't think from that that I knew what the score was. War correspondents have told me of the frustrating life they led at some close-mouthed commands. Soandso-many air sorties, the largest number since January fifteenth. Casualties a full fifteen per cent lighter than expected. Determined advance in an active sector against relatively strong enemy opposition. And so on—all adding up to nothing in the way of real information.

That's what it was like in my diary because that's all they told me. Here are some excerpts: "On the recommendation of Dr. Mines, Mr. Gomez today began work on a phase of reactor design theory to be implemented at Brookhaven National Laboratory. The work involves the setting-up of thirty-five pairs of partial differential equations . . . Mr. Gomez announced tentatively today that in checking certain theoretical work in progress at the Los Alamos Laboratory of the A.E.C. he discovered a fallacious assumption concerning neutron-spin which invalidates the conclusions reached. This will be communicated to the Laboratory . . . Dr. Mines said today that Mr. Gomez has successfully invoked a hitherto-unexploited aspect of Minkowski's tensor analysis to crack a stubborn obstacle towards the control of thermonuclear reactions . . ."

I protested at one of the briefing sessions with Dr. Mines against this gobbledegook. He didn't mind my protesting. He leaned back in his chair and said calmly: "Vilchek, with all friendliness I assure you that you're getting everything you can understand. Anything more complex than the vague description of what's going on would be over your head. And anything more specific would give away exact engineering information which would be of use to foreign countries."

"This isn't the way they treated Bill Lawrence when he covered the atomic bomb," I said bitterly.

Mines nodded, with a pleased smile. "That's it exactly," he said. "Broad principles were being developed then—interesting things that could be told without any great harm being done. If you tell somebody that a critical mass of U-235 or Plutonium goes off with a big bang, you really haven't given away a great deal. He still has millions of man-hours of engineering before him to figure out how much is critical mass, to take only one small point."

So I took his word for it, faithfully copied the communiques he gave me and wrote what I could on the human-interest side for release some day.

So I recorded Gomez' progress with English, his taste for chicken pot pie and rice pudding, his habit of doing his own housework on the top floor and his old-maidish neatness. "You live your first fifteen years in a tin shack, Beel," he told me once, "and you find out you like things nice and clean." I've seen Dr. Mines follow Gomez through the top floor as the boy swept and dusted, talking at him in their mathematical jargon.

Gomez worked in forty-eight hour spells usually, and not eating much. Then for a couple of days he'd live like a human being grabbing naps, playing catch on the lawn with one or another of the Security people, talking with me about his childhood in Puerto Rico and his youth in New York. He taught me a little Spanish and asked me to catch him up on bad mistakes in English.

"But don't you ever want to get out of here?" I demanded one day.

He grinned: "Why should I, Beel? Here I eat good, I can send money to the parents. Best, I find out what the big professors are up to without I have to wait five-ten years for damn de-classifying."

"Don't you have a girl?"

He was embarrassed and changed the subject back to the big professors.

Dr. Mines drove up then, with his chauffeur who looked like a G-man and almost certainly was. As usual, the physicist was toting a bulging briefcase. After a few polite words with me, he and Julio went indoors and upstairs.

They were closeted for five hours—a record. When Dr. Mines came down I expected the usual briefing session. But he begged off. "Nothing serious," he said. "We just sat down and kicked some ideas of his around. I told him to go ahead. We've been—ah—using him very much like a sort of computer, you know. Turning him loose on the problems that were too tough for me and some of the other men. He's got the itch for research now. It would be very interesting if his forte turned out to be creative."

I agreed.

Julio didn't come down for dinner. I woke up in darkness that night when there was a loud bump overhead, and went upstairs in my pyjamas.

Gomez was sprawled, fully dressed, on the floor. He'd tripped over a footstool. And he didn't seem to have noticed. His lips were moving and he stared straight at me without knowing I was there.

"You all right, Julio?" I asked, and started to help him to his feet.

He got up mechanically and said: "—real values of the zeta function vanish."

"How's that?"

He saw me then and asked, puzzled: "How you got in here, Beel? Is dinnertime?"

"Is four A.M., *por dios*. Don't you think you ought to get some sleep?" He looked terrible.

No; he didn't think he ought to get some sleep. He had some work to do. I went downstairs and heard him pacing overhead for an hour until I dozed off.

This splurge of work didn't wear off in forty-eight hours. For a week I brought him meals and sometimes he ate absently, with one hand, as he scribbled on a yellow pad. Sometimes I'd bring him lunch to find his breakfast untouched. He didn't have much beard, but he let it grow for a week—too busy to shave, too busy to talk, too busy to eat, sleeping in chairs when fatigue caught up with him.

I asked Leitzer, badly worried, if we should do anything about it. He had a direct scrambler-phone connection with the New York Security and Intelligence office, but his orders didn't cover anything like a self-induced nervous breakdown of the man he was guarding.

I thought Dr. Mines would do something when he came—call in an M.D., or tell Gomez to take it easy, or take some of the load off by parcelling out whatever he had by the tail.

But he didn't. He went upstairs, came down two hours later and absently tried to walk past me. I headed him off into my room. "What's the word?" I demanded.

He looked me in the eye and said defiantly: "He's doing fine. I don't want to stop him."

Dr. Mines was a good man. Dr. Mines was a humane man. And he wouldn't lift a finger to keep the boy from working himself into nervous prostration. Dr. Mines liked people well enough, but he reserved his love for theoretical physics. "How important can this thing be?"

He shrugged irritably. "It's just the way some scientists work," he said. "Newton was like that. So was Sir William Rowan Hamilton—"

"Hamilton-Schmamilton," I said. "What's the sense of it? *Why* doesn't he sleep or eat?"

Mines said: *"You* don't know what it's like."

"Of course," I said, getting good and sore. "I'm just a dumb newspaper man. Tell me, Mr. Bones, what is it like?"

There was a long pause, and he said mildly: "I'll try. That boy up there is using his brain. A great chess player can put on a blindfold and play a hundred opponents in a hundred games simultaneously, remembering all the positions of his pieces and theirs and keeping a hundred strategies clear in his mind. Well, that stunt simply isn't in the same league with what Julio's doing up there.

"He has in his head some millions of facts concerning theoretical physics. He's scanning them, picking out one here and there, fitting them into new relationships, checking and rejecting when he has to, fitting the new relationships together, turning them upside-down and inside-out to see what happens, comparing them with known doctrine, holding them in his memory while he repeats the whole process and compares —and all the while he has a goal firmly in mind against which he's measuring all these things." He seemed to be finished.

For a reporter, I felt strangely shy. "What's he driving at?" I asked.

"I think," he said slowly, "he's approaching a unified field theory."

Apparently that was supposed to explain everything. I let Dr. Mines know that it didn't.

He said thoughtfully: "I don't know whether I can get it over to a layman—no offense, Vilchek. Let's put it this way. You know how math comes in waves, and how it's followed by waves of applied science based on the math. There was a big wave of algebra in the middle ages—following it came navigation, gunnery, surveying and so on. Then the renaissance and a wave of analysis—what you'd call calculus. That opened up steam power and how to use it, mechanical engineering, electricity. The wave of *modern* mathematics since say 1875 gave us atomic energy. That boy upstairs may be starting off the next big wave."

He got up and reached for his hat.

"Just a minute," I said. I was surprised that my voice was steady. "What comes next? Control of gravity? Control of personality? Sending people by radio?"

Dr. Mines wouldn't meet my eye. Suddenly he looked old and shrunken. "Don't worry about the boy," he said.

I let him go.

That evening I brought Gomez chicken pot pie and a non-alcoholic egg nog. He drank the egg nog, said "Hi, Beel," and continued to cover yellow sheets of paper.

I went downstairs and worried.

Abruptly it ended late the next afternoon. Gomez wandered into the big first-floor kitchen looking like a starved old rickshaw coolie. He pushed his lank hair back from his forehead, said: "Beel, what is to eat—" and pitched forward onto the linoleum. Leitzer came when I yelled, expertly took Gomez' pulse, rolled him onto a blanket and threw another one over him. "It's just a faint," he said. "Let's get him to bed."

"Aren't you going to call a doctor, man?"

"Doctor couldn't do anything we can't do," he said stolidly. "And I'm here to see that security isn't breached. Give me a hand."

We got him upstairs and put him to bed. He woke up and said something in Spanish, and then, apologetically: "Very sorry, fellows. I ought to taken it easier."

"I'll get you some lunch," I said, and he grinned.

He ate it all, enjoying it heartily, and finally lay back gorged. "Well," he asked me, "what it is new, Beel?"

"What *is* new. And you should tell me. You finish your work?"

"I got it in shape to finish. The hard part it is over." He rolled out of bed.

"Hey!" I said.

"I'm okay now," he grinned. "Don't write this down in your history, Beel. Everybody will think I act like a woman."

I followed him into his work room where he flopped into an easy chair, his eyes on a blackboard covered with figures. He wasn't grinning any more.

"Dr. Mines says you're up to something big," I said.

"*Si*. Big."

"Unified field theory, he says."

"That is it," Gomez said.

"Is it good or bad?" I asked, licking my lips. "The application, I mean."

His boyish mouth set suddenly in a grim line. "That, it is not my business," he said. "I am American citizen of the United States." He stared at the blackboard and its maze of notes.

I looked at it too—*really* looked at it for once—and was surprised by what I saw. Mathematics, of course, I don't know. But I had soaked up a very little *about* mathematics. One of the things I had soaked up was that the expressions of higher mathematics tend to be complicated and elaborate, involving English, Greek and Hebrew letters, plain and fancy brackets and a great variety of special signs besides the plus and minus of the elementary school.

The things on the blackboard weren't like that at all. The board was covered with variations of a simple expression that consisted of five letters and two symbols: a right-handed pothook and a left-handed pothook.

"What do they mean?" I asked, pointing.

"Somethings I made up," he said nervously. "The word for that one is 'enfields.' The other one is 'is enfielded by.' "

"What's *that* mean?"

His luminous eyes were haunted. He didn't answer.

"It looks like simple stuff. I read somewhere that all the basic stuff is simple once it's been discovered."

"Yes," he said almost inaudibly. "It is simple, Beel. Too

damn simple, I think. Better I carry it in my head, I think."
He strode to the blackboard and erased it. Instinctively I half-
rose to stop him. He gave me a grin that was somehow bitter
and unlike him. "Don't worry," he said. "I don't forget it."
He tapped his forehead. "I *can't* forget it." I hope I never see
again on any face the look that was on his.

"Julio," I said, appalled. "Why don't you get out of here for
a while? Why don't you run over to New York and see your
folks and have some fun? They can't keep you here against
your will."

"They told me I shouldn't—" he said uncertainly. And
then he got tough. "You're damn right, Beel. Let's go in together. I get dressed up. Er—You tell Leitzer, hah?" He
couldn't quite face up to the hard-boiled security man.

I told Leitzer, who hit the ceiling. But all it boiled down to
was that he sincerely wished Gomez and I wouldn't leave.
We weren't in the Army, we weren't in jail. I got hot at last
and yelled back that we were damn well going out and he
couldn't stop us. He called New York on his direct wire and
apparently New York confirmed it, regretfully.

We got on the 4:05 Jersey Central, with Higgins and Dalhousie tailing us at a respectful distance. Gomez didn't notice
them and I didn't tell him. He was having too much fun. He
had a shine put on his shoes at Penn Station and worried about
the taxi fare as we rode up to Spanish Harlem.

His parents lived in a neat little three-room apartment. A
lot of the furniture looked brand-new, and I was pretty sure
who had paid for it. The mother and father spoke only Spanish, and mumbled shyly when *"mi amigo Beel"* was introduced. I had a very halting conversation with the father while
the mother and Gomez rattled away happily and she poked
his ribs to point up the age-old complaint of any mother anywhere that he wasn't eating enough.

The father, of course, thought the boy was a janitor or
something in the Pentagon and, as near as I could make out,
he was worried about his Julio being grabbed off by a man-
hungry government girl. I kept reassuring him that his Julio
was a good boy, a very good boy, and he seemed to get some
comfort out of it.

There was a little spat when his mother started to set the
table. Gomez said reluctantly that we couldn't stay, that we
were eating somewhere else. His mother finally dragged from

him the admission that we were going to the Porto Bello so he could see Rosa, and everything was smiles again. The father told me that Rosa was a good girl, a very good girl.

Walking down the three flights of stairs with yelling little kids playing tag around us, Gomez asked proudly: "You not think they in America only a little time, hey?"

I yanked him around by the elbow as we went down the brownstone stoop into the street. Otherwise he would have seen our shadows for sure. I didn't want to spoil his fun.

The Porto Bello was full, and the pretty little girl was on duty as cashier at the table. Gomez got a last-minute attack of cold feet at the sight of her. "No table," he said. "We better go someplace else."

I practically dragged him in. "We'll get a table in a minute," I said.

"Julio," said the girl, when she saw him.

He looked sheepish. "Hello, Rosa. I'm back for a while."

"I'm glad to see you again," she said tremulously.

"I'm glad to see you again too—" I nudged him. "Rosa, this is my good friend Beel. We work together in Washington."

"Pleased to meet you, Rosa. Can you have dinner with us? I'll bet you and Julio have a lot to talk over."

"Well, I'll see . . . look, there's a table for you. I'll see if I can get away."

We sat down and she flagged down the proprietress and got away in a hurry.

All three of us had *arróz con pollo*—rice with chicken and lots of other things. Their shyness wore off and I was dealt out of the conversation, but I didn't mind. They were a nice young couple. I liked the way they smiled at each other, and the things they remembered happily—movies, walks, talks. It made me feel like a benevolent uncle with one foot in the grave. It made me forget for a while the look on Gomez' face when he turned from the blackboard he had covered with too-simple math.

Over dessert I broke in. By then they were unselfconsciously holding hands. "Look," I said, "why don't you two go on and do the town? Julio, I'll be at the Madison Park Hotel." I scribbled the address and gave it to him. "And I'll get a room for you. Have fun and reel in any time." I rapped his knee. He looked down and I slipped him four twenties. I didn't know whether he had money on him or not, but anything extra the boy could use he had coming to him.

"Swell," he said. "Thanks." And looked shame-faced while I looked paternal.

I had been watching a young man who was moodily eating alone in a corner, reading a paper. He was about Julio's height and build and he wore a sports jacket pretty much like Julio's. And the street was pretty dark outside.

The young man got up moodily and headed for the cashier's table. "Gotta go," I said. "Have fun."

I went out of the restaurant right behind the young man and walked as close behind him as I dared, hoping we were being followed.

After a block and a half of this, he turned on me and snarled: "Wadda you, mister? A wolf? Beat it!"

"Okay," I said mildly, and turned and walked the other way. Higgins and Dalhousie were standing there, flat-footed and open-mouthed. They sprinted back to the Porto Bello, and *I* followed *them*. But Julio and Rosa had already left.

"Tough, fellows," I said to them as they stood in the doorway. They looked as if they wanted to murder me. "He won't get into any trouble," I said. "He's just going out with his girl." Dalhousie made a strangled noise and told Higgins: "Cruise around the neighborhood. See if you can pick them up. I'll follow Vilchek." He wouldn't talk to me. I shrugged and got a cab and went to the Madison Park Hotel, a pleasantly un-fashionable old place with big rooms where I stay when business brings me to New York. They had a couple of adjoining singles; I took one in my own name and the other for Gomez.

I wandered around the neighborhood for a while and had a couple of beers in one of the ultra-Irish bars on Third Avenue. After a pleasant argument with a gent who thought the Russians didn't have any atomic bombs and faked their demonstrations and that we ought to blow up their industrial cities tomorrow at dawn, I went back to the hotel.

I didn't get to sleep easily. The citizen who didn't believe Russia could maul the United States pretty badly or at all had started me thinking again—all kinds of ugly thoughts. Dr. Mines who had turned into a shrunken old man at the men-tion of applying Gomez' work. The look on the boy's face. My layman's knowledge that present-day "atomic energy" taps only the smallest fragment of the energy locked up in the atom. My layman's knowledge that once genius has broken a trail in science, mediocrity can follow the trail.

But I slept at last, for three hours.

At four-fifteen A.M. according to my watch the telephone rang long and hard. There was some switchboard and long-distance-operator mumbo-jumbo and then Julio's gleeful voice: "Beel! Congratulate us. We got marriage!"

"Married," I said fuzzily. "You got *married,* not marriage. How's that again?"

"We got *married.* Me and Rosa. We get on the train, the taxi driver takes us to justice of peace, we got *married,* we go to hotel here."

"Congratulations," I said, waking up. "Lots of congratulations. But you're under age, there's a waiting period—"

"Not in this state," he chuckled. "Here is no waiting periods and here I have twenty-one years if I say so."

"Well," I said. "Lots of congratulations, Julio. And tell Rosa she's got herself a good boy."

"Thanks, Beel," he said shyly. "I call you so you don't worry when I don't come in tonight. I think I come in with Rosa tomorrow so we tell her mama and my mama and papa. I call you at the hotel, I still have the piece of paper."

"Okay, Julio. All the best. Don't worry about a thing." I hung up, chuckling, and went right back to sleep.

Well, sir, it happened again.

I was shaken out of my sleep by the strong, skinny hand of Admiral MacDonald. It was seven-thirty and a bright New York morning. Dalhousie had pulled a blank canvassing the neighborhood for Gomez, got panicky and bucked it up to higher headquarters.

"Where is he?" the Admiral rasped.

"On his way here with his bride of one night," I said. "He slipped over a couple of state lines and got married."

"By God," the admiral said, "we've got to do something about this. I'm going to have him drafted and assigned to special duty. This is the last time—"

"*Look,*" I said. "You've got to stop treating him like a chesspiece. You've got duty-honor-country on the brain and thank God for that. Somebody has to; it's your profession. But can't you get it through your head that Gomez is a kid and that you're wrecking his life by forcing him to grind out science like a machine? And I'm just a stupe of a layman, but have you professionals worried once about digging too deep and blowing up the whole shebang?"

He gave me a piercing look and said nothing.

I dressed and had breakfast sent up. The admiral, Dalhousie and I waited grimly until noon, and then Gomez phoned up.

"Come on up, Julio," I said tiredly.

He breezed in with his blushing bride on his arm. The admiral rose automatically as she entered, and immediately began tongue-lashing the boy. He spoke more in sorrow than in anger. He made it clear that Gomez wasn't treating his country right. That he had a great talent and it belonged to the United States. That his behavior had been irresponsible. That Gomez would have to come to heel and realize that his wishes weren't the most important thing in his life. That he could and would be drafted if there were any more such escapades.

"As a starter, Mr. Gomez," the admiral snapped, "I want you to set down, immediately, the enfieldment matrices you have developed. I consider it almost criminal of you to arrogantly and carelessly trust to your memory alone matters of such vital importance. Here!" He thrust pencil and paper at the boy, who stood, drooping and disconsolate. Little Rosa was near crying. She didn't have the ghost of a notion as to what it was about.

Gomez took the pencil and paper and sat down at the writing table silently. I took Rosa by the arm. She was trembling. "It's all right," I said. "They can't do a thing to him." The admiral glared briefly at me and then returned his gaze to Gomez.

The boy made a couple of tentative marks. Then his eyes went wide and he clutched his hair. *"Dios mio!"* he said. *"Esta perdido! Olvidado!"*

Which means: "My God, it's lost! Forgotten!"

The admiral turned white beneath his tan. "Now, boy," he said slowly and soothingly. "I didn't mean to scare you. You just relax and collect yourself. Of course you haven't forgotten, not with that memory of yours. Start with something easy. Write down a general biquadratic equation, say."

Gomez just looked at him. After a long pause he said in a strangled voice: *"No puedo.* I can't. It too I forget. I don't

think of the math or physics at all since—" He looked at
Rosa and turned a little red. She smiled shyly and looked at
her shoes.

"That is it," Gomez said hoarsely. "Not since then. Always
before in the back of my head is the math, but not since then."

"My God," the admiral said softly. "Can such a thing happen?" He reached for the phone.

He found out that such things can happen.

Julio went back to Spanish Harlem and bought a piece of
the Porto Bello with his savings. I went back to the paper
and bought a car with *my* savings. MacDonald never cleared
the story, so the Sunday editor had the satisfaction of bull-
dozing an admiral, but didn't get his exclusive.

Julio and Rosa sent me a card eventually announcing the
birth of their first-born: a six-pound boy, Francisco, named after Julio's father. I saved the card and when a New York assignment came my way—it was the National Association of
Dry Goods Wholesalers; dry goods are important in our town
—I dropped up to see them.

Julio was a little more mature and a little more prosperous.
Rosa—alas!—was already putting on weight, but she was
still a pretty thing and devoted to her man. The baby was a
honey-skinned little wiggler. It was nice to see all of them
together, happy with their lot.

Julio insisted that he'd cook *arróz con pollo* for me, as on
the night I practically threw him into Rosa's arms, but he'd
have to shop for the stuff. I went along.

In the corner grocery he ordered the rice, the chicken, the
garbanzos, the peppers and, swept along by the enthusiasm
that hits husbands in groceries, about fifty other things that
he thought would be nice to have in the pantry.

The creaking old grocer scribbled down the prices on a
shopping bag and began painfully to add them up while Julio
was telling me how well the Porto Bello was doing and how
they were thinking of renting the adjoining store.

"Seventeen dollars, forty-two cents," the grocer said at last.

Julio flicked one glance at the shopping bag and the upside-
down figures. "Should be seventeen thirty-nine," he said re-
provingly. "Add up again."

The grocer painfully added up again and said. "Is seventeen

thirty-nine. Sorry." He began to pack the groceries into the bag.

"Hey," I said.

We didn't discuss it then or ever. Julio just said: "Don't tell, Beel." And winked.

The Mindworm

THE handsome j. g. and the pretty nurse held out against it as long as they reasonably could, but blue Pacific water, languid tropical nights and the low atoll dreaming on the horizon—and the complete absence of any other nice young people for company on the small, uncomfortable parts boat —did their work. On June 30th they watched through dark glasses as the dazzling thing burst over the fleet and the atoll. Her manicured hand gripped his arm in excitement and terror. Unfelt radiation sleeted through their loins.

A storekeeper-third-class named Bielaski watched the young couple with more interest than he showed in Test Able. After all, he had twenty-five dollars riding on the nurse. That night he lost it to a chief bosun's mate who had backed the j. g.

In the course of time, the careless nurse was discharged under conditions other than honorable. The j. g., who didn't like to put things in writing, phoned her all the way from Manila to say it was a damned shame. When her gratitude gave way to specific inquiry, their overseas connection went bad and he had to hang up.

She had a child, a boy, turned it over to a foundling home and vanished from his life into a series of good jobs and finally marriage.

The boy grew up stupid, puny and stubborn, greedy and miserable. To the home's hilarious young athletics director he suddenly said: "You hate me. You think I make the rest of the boys look bad."

The athletics director blustered and laughed, and later told the doctor over coffee: "I watch myself around the kids.

27

They're sharp—they catch a look or a gesture and it's like a blow in the face to them, I know that, so I watch myself. So how did he know?"

The doctor told the boy: "Three pounds more this month isn't bad, but how about you pitch in and clean up your plate *every* day? Can't live on meat and water; those vegetables make you big and strong."

The boy said: "What's 'neurasthenic' mean?"

The doctor later said to the director: "It made my flesh creep. I was looking at his little spindling body and dishing out the old pep-talk about growing big and strong, and inside my head I was thinking 'we'd call him neurasthenic in the old days' and then out he popped with it. What should we do? Should we do anything? Maybe it'll go away. I don't know anything about these things. I don't know whether anybody does."

"Reads minds, does he?" asked the director. *Be damned if he's going to read my mind about Schultz Meat Market's ten per cent.* "Doctor, I think I'm going to take my vacation a little early this year. Has anybody shown any interest in adopting the child?"

"Not him. He wasn't a baby-doll when we got him, and at present he's an exceptionally unattractive-looking kid. You know how people don't give a damn about anything but their looks."

"*Some* couples would take anything, or so they tell me."

"Unapproved for foster-parenthood, you mean?"

"Red tape and arbitrary classifications sometimes limit us too severely in our adoptions."

"If you're going to wish him on some screwball couple that the courts turned down as unfit, I want no part of it."

"You don't have to have any part of it, doctor. By the way, which dorm does he sleep in?"

"West," grunted the doctor, leaving the office.

The director called a few friends—a judge, a couple the judge referred him to, a court clerk. Then he left by way of the east wing of the building.

The boy survived three months with the Berrymans. Hard-drinking Mimi alternately caressed and shrieked at him; Edward W. tried to be a good scout and just gradually lost interest, looking clean through him. He hit the road in June and got by with it for a while. He wore a Boy Scout uniform,

and Boy Scouts can turn up anywhere, any time. The money
he had taken with him lasted a month. When the last penny of
the last dollar was three days spent, he was adrift on a
Nebraska prairie. He had walked out of the last small town
because the constable was beginning to wonder what on earth
he was hanging around for and who he belonged to. The town
was miles behind on the two-lane highway; the infrequent cars
did not stop.

One of Nebraska's "rivers", a dry bed at this time of year,
lay ahead, spanned by a railroad culvert. There were some
men in its shade, and he was hungry.

They were ugly, dirty men, and their thoughts were
muddled and stupid. They called him "Shorty" and gave him a
little dirty bread and some stinking sardines from a can. The
thoughts of one of them became less muddled and uglier.
He talked to the rest out of the boy's hearing, and they
whooped with laughter. The boy got ready to run, but his
legs wouldn't hold him up.

He could read the thoughts of the men quite clearly as they
headed for him. Outrage, fear and disgust blended in him and
somehow turned inside-out and one of the men was dead on
the dry ground, grasshoppers vaulting onto his flannel shirt,
the others backing away, frightened now, not frightening.

He wasn't hungry any more; he felt quite comfortable and
satisfied. He got up and headed for the other men, who ran.
The rearmost of them was thinking *Jeez he folded up the evil
eye we was only gonna—*

Again the boy let the thoughts flow into his head and again
he flipped his own thoughts around them; it was quite easy to
do. It was different—this man's terror from the other's lustful
anticipation. But both had their points. . . .

At his leisure, he robbed the bodies of three dollars and
twenty-four cents.

Thereafter his fame preceded him like a death-wind. Two
years on the road and he had his growth, and his fill of the
dull and stupid minds he met there. He moved to northern
cities, a year here, a year there, quiet, unobtrusive, prudent,
an epicure.

Sebastian Long woke suddenly, with something on his mind.
As night-fog cleared away he remembered, happily. Today
he started the Demeter Bowl! At last there was time, at last

there was money—six hundred and twenty-three dollars in the bank. He had packed and shipped the three dozen cocktail glasses last night, engraved with Mrs. Klausman's initials—his last commercial order for as many months as the Bowl would take.

He shifted from nightshirt to denims, gulped coffee, boiled an egg but was too excited to eat it. He went to the front of his shop-workroom-apartment, checked the lock, waved at neighbors' children on their way to school, and ceremoniously set a sign in the cluttered window.

It said: "NO COMMERCIAL ORDERS TAKEN UNTIL FURTHER NOTICE."

From a closet he tenderly carried a shrouded object that made a double armful and laid it on his workbench. Unshrouded, it was a glass bowl—*what* a glass bowl! The clearest Swedish lead glass, the purest lines he had even seen, his secret treasure since the crazy day he had bought it, long ago, for six months' earnings. His wife had given him hell for that until the day she died. From the closet he brought a portfolio filled with sketches and designs dating back to the day he had bought the bowl. He smiled over the first, excitedly scrawled—a florid, rococo conception, unsuited to the classicism of the lines and the serenity of the perfect glass.

Through many years and hundreds of sketches he had refined his conception to the point where it was, he humbly felt, not unsuited to the medium. A strongly-molded Demeter was to dominate the piece, a matron as serene as the glass, and all the fruits of the earth would flow from her gravely outstretched arms.

Suddenly and surely, he began to work. With a candle he thinly smoked an oval area on the outside of the bowl. Two steady fingers clipped the Demeter drawing against the carbon black; a hair-fine needle in his other hand traced her lines. When the transfer of the design was done, Sebastian Long readied his lathe. He fitted a small copper wheel, slightly worn as he liked them, into the chuck and with his fingers charged it with the finest rouge from Rouen. He took an ashtray cracked in delivery and held it against the spinning disk. It bit in smoothly, with the *wiping* feel to it that was exactly right.

Holding out his hands, seeing that the fingers did not tremble with excitement, he eased the great bowl to the lathe and was about to make the first tiny cut of the millions that would go into the masterpiece.

Somebody knocked on his door and rattled the doorknob.

Sebastian Long did not move or look toward the door. Soon the busybody would read the sign and go away. But the pounding and the rattling of the knob went on. He eased down the bowl and angrily went to the window, picked up the sign and shook it at whoever it was—he couldn't make out the face very well. But the idiot wouldn't go away.

The engraver unlocked the door, opened it a bit and snapped: "The shop is closed. I shall not be taking any orders for several months. Please don't bother me now."

"It's about the Demeter Bowl," said the intruder.

Sebastian Long stared at him. "What the devil do you know about my Demeter Bowl?" He saw the man was a stranger, undersized by a little, middle-aged. . . .

"Just let me in please," urged the man. "It's important. Please!"

"I don't know what your talking about," said the engraver. "But what do you know about my Demeter Bowl?" He hooked his thumbs pugnaciously over the waistband of his denims and glowered at the stranger. The stranger promptly took advantage of his hand being removed from the door and glided in.

Sebastian Long thought briefly that it might be a nightmare as the man darted quickly about his shop, picking up a graver and throwing it down, picking up a wire scratch-wheel and throwing it down. "Here, you!" he roared, as the stranger picked up a crescent wrench which he did not throw down.

As Long started for him, the stranger darted to the workbench and brought the crescent wrench down shatteringly on the bowl.

Sebastian Long's heart was bursting with sorrow and rage; such a storm of emotions as he never had known thundered through him. Paralyzed, he saw the stranger smile with anticipation.

The engraver's legs folded under him and he fell to the floor, drained and dead.

The Mindworm, locked in the bedroom of his brownstone front, smiled again, reminiscently.

Smiling, he checked the day on a wall calendar.

"Dolores!" yelled her mother in Spanish. "Are you going to pass the whole day in there?"

She had been practicing low-lidded, sexy half-smiles like Lauren Bacall in the bathroom mirror. She stormed out and yelled in English: "I don't know how many times I tell you not to call me that Spick name no more!"

"Dolly!" sneered her mother. "Dah-lee! When was there a Saint Dah-lee that you call yourself after, eh?"

The girl snarled a Spanish obscenity at her mother and ran down the tenement stairs. Jeez, she was gonna be late for sure!

Held up by a stream of traffic between her and her streetcar, she danced with impatience. Then the miracle happened. Just like in the movies, a big convertible pulled up before her and its lounging driver said, opening the door: "You seem to be in a hurry. Could I drop you somewhere?"

Dazed at the sudden realization of a hundred daydreams, she did not fail to give the driver a low-lidded, sexy smile as she said: "Why, *thanks!*" and climbed in. He wasn't no Cary Grant, but he had all his hair . . . kind of small, but so was she . . . and jeez, the convertible had *leopard-skin seat covers!*

The car was in the stream of traffic, purring down the avenue. "It's a lovely day," she said. "Really too nice to work."

The driver smiled shyly, kind of like Jimmy Stewart but of course not so tall, and said: "I feel like playing hooky myself. How would you like a spin down Long Island?"

"Be wonderful!" The convertible cut left on an odd-numbered street.

"Play hooky, you said. What do you do?"

"Advertising."

"Advertising!" Dolly wanted to kick herself for ever having doubted, for ever having thought in low, self-loathing moments that it wouldn't work out, that she'd marry a grocer or a mechanic and live forever after in a smelly tenement and grow old and sick and stooped. She felt vaguely in her happy daze that it might have been cuter, she might have accidentally pushed him into a pond or something, but this was cute enough. An advertising man, leopard-skin seat covers . . . what more could a girl with a sexy smile and a nice little figure want?

Speeding down the South Shore she learned that his name was Michael Brent, exactly as it ought to be. She wished she could tell him she was Jennifer Brown or one of those real cute names they had nowadays, but was reassured when he told her he thought Dolly Gonzalez was a beautiful name. He didn't, and she noticed the omission, add: "It's the most beautiful name I ever heard!" That, she comfortably thought as she settled herself against the cushions, would come later.

They stopped at Medford for lunch, a wonderful lunch in a little restaurant where you went down some steps and there were candles on the table. She called him "Michael" and he called her "Dolly." She learned that he liked dark girls and thought the stories in *True Story* really were true, and that he thought she was just tall enough, and that Greer Garson was wonderful, but not the way she was, and that he thought her dress was just wonderful.

They drove slowly after Medford, and Michael Brent did most of the talking. He had traveled all over the world. He had been in the war and wounded—just a flesh wound. He was 38, and had been married once, but she died. There were no children. He was alone in the world. He had nobody to share his town house in the 50's, his country place in Westchester, his lodge in the Maine woods. Every word sent the girl floating higher and higher on a tide of happiness; the signs were unmistakable.

When they reached Montauk Point, the last sandy bit of the continent before blue water and Europe, it was sunset, with a great wrinkled sheet of purple and rose stretching half across the sky and the first stars appearing above the dark horizon of the water.

The two of them walked from the parked car out onto the sand, alone, bathed in glorious Technicolor. Her heart was nearly bursting with joy as she heard Michael Brent say, his arms tightening around her: "Darling, will you marry me?"

"Oh, *yes* Michael!" she breathed, dying.

The Mindworm, drowsing, suddenly felt the sharp sting of danger. He cast out through the great city, dragging tentacles of thought:

". . . die if she don't let me . . ."

". . . six an' six is twelve an' carry one an' three is four . . ."

". . . gobblegobble madre de dios pero soy gobblegobble . . ."

". . . parlay Domino an' Missab and shoot the roll on Duchess Peg in the feature . . ."

". . . melt resin add the silver chloride and dissolve in oil of lavender stand and decant and fire to cone 012 give you shimmering streaks of luster down the walls . . ."

". . . moiderin' square-headed gobblegobble tried ta poke his eye out wassamatta witta ref . . ."

". . . O God I am most heartily sorry I have offended thee in . . ."

". . . talk like a commie . . ."

". . . gobblegobblegobble two dolla twenny-fi' sense gobble . . ."

". . . just a nip and fill it up with water and brush my teeth . . ."

". . . really know I'm God but fear to confess their sins . . ."

". . . dirty lousy rock-headed claw-handed paddle-footed goggle-eyed snot-nosed hunch-backed feeble-minded pot-bellied son of . . ."

". . . write on the wall alfie is a stunkur and then . . ."

". . . thinks I believe it's a television set but I know he's got a bomb in there but who can I tell who can help so alone . . ."

". . . gabble was ich weiss nicht gabble geh bei Broadvay gabble . . ."

". . . habt mein daughter Rosie such a fella gobblegobble . . ."

". . . wonder if that's one didn't look back . . ."

". . . seen with her in the Medford restaurant . . ."

The Mindworm struck into that thought.

". . . not a mark on her but the M. E.'s have been wrong before and heart failure don't mean a thing anyway try to talk to her old lady authorize an autopsy get Pancho little guy talks Spanish be best . . ."

The Mindworm knew he would have to be moving again—soon. He was sorry; some of the thoughts he had tapped indicated good . . . hunting?

Regretfully, he again dragged his net:

". . . with chartreuse drinks I mean drapes could use a drink come to think of it . . ."

". . . reep-beep-reep-beep reepiddy-beepiddy-beep bop man wadda beat . . ."

ˌˀᵌˣᵣₙˀˣ₍ₙ₎ˤₒ ˀᵍ₍ˀˣ₁ˣₗₐ,ⁱ⁻ₒ *What the Hell was that?"*

The Mindworm withdrew, in frantic haste. The intelligence was massive, its overtones those of a vigorous adult. He had learned from certain dangerous children that there was peril of a leveling flow. Shaken and scared, he contemplated traveling. He would need more than that wretched girl had supplied, and it would not be epicurean. There would be no time to find individuals at a ripe emotional crisis, or goad them to one. It would be plain—munching. The Mindworm drank a glass of water, also necessary to his metabolism.

EIGHT FOUND DEAD
IN UPTOWN MOVIE;
"MOLESTER" SOUGHT

Eight persons, including three women, were found dead Wednesday night of unknown causes in widely-separated seats in the balcony of the Odeon Theater at 117th St. and Broadway. Police are seeking a man described by the balcony usher, Michael Fenelly, 18, as "acting like a woman-molester."

Fenelly discovered the first of the fatalities after seeing the man "moving from one empty seat to another several times." He went to ask a woman in a seat next to one the man had just vacated whether he had annoyed her. She was dead.

Almost at once, a scream rang out. In another part of the balcony Mrs. Sadie Rabinowitz, 40, uttered the cry when another victim toppled from his seat next to her.

Theater manager I. J. Marcusohn stopped the show and turned on the house lights. He tried to instruct his staff to keep the audience from leaving before the police arrived. He failed to get word to them in time, however, and most of the audience was gone when a detail from the 24th Pct. and an ambulance from Harlem hospital took over at the scene of the tragedy.

The Medical Examiner's office has not yet made a report as to the causes of death. A spokesman said the victims showed no signs of poisoning or violence. He added that it "was inconceivable that it could be a coincidence."

Lt. John Braidwood of the 24th Pct. said of the alleged molester: "We got a fair description of him and naturally we will try to bring him in for questioning."

Clickety-click, clickety-click, clickety-click sang the rails as the Mindworm drowsed in his coach seat.

Some people were walking forward from the diner. One was thinking: "Different-looking fellow. (a) he's aberrant. (b) he's nonaberrant and ill. Cancel (b)—respiration normal, skin smooth and healthy, no tremor of limbs, well-groomed. Is aberrant (1) trivially. (2) significantly. Cancel (1)—displayed no involuntary interest when . . . odd! *Running* for the washroom! Unexpected because (a) neat grooming indicates amour propre inconsistent with amusing others; (b) evident health inconsistent with . . ." It had taken one second, was fully detailed.

The Mindworm, locked in the toilet of the coach, wondered what the next stop was. He was getting off at it—not frightened, just careful. Dodge them, keep dodging them and everything would be all right. Send out no mental taps until the train was far away and everything would be all right.

He got off at a West Virginia coal and iron town surrounded by ruined mountains and filled with the offscourings of Eastern Europe. Serbs, Albanians, Croats, Hungarians, Slovenes, Bulgarians and all possible combinations and permutations thereof. He walked slowly from the smoke-stained, brownstone passenger station. The train had roared on its way.

". . . ain' no gemmum that's fo sho', fi-cen' tip fo' a good shine lak ah give um . . ."

". . . dumb bassar don't know how to make out a billa lading yet he ain't never gonna know so fire him get it over with . . ."

". . . gabblegabblegabble . . ." Not a word he recognized in it.

". . . gobblegobble dat tam vooman I brek she nack . . ."

". . . gobble trink visky chin glassabeer gobblegobblegobble . . ."

". . . gabblegabblegabble . . ."

". . . makes me so gobblegobble mad little no-good tramp no she ain' but I don' like no standup from no dame . . ."

A blond, square-headed boy fuming under a street light.

". . . out wit' Casey Oswiak I could kill that dumb bohunk alla time trine ta paw her . . ."

It was a possibility. The Mindworm drew near.

". . . stand me up for that gobblegobble bohunk I oughtta slap her inna mush like my ole man says . . ."

"Hello," said the Mindworm.

"Waddaya wan'?"

"Casey Oswiak told me to tell you not to wait up for your girl. He's taking her out tonight."

The blond boy's rage boiled into his face and shot from his eyes. He was about to swing when the Mindworm began to feed. It was like pheasant after chicken, venison after beef. The coarseness of the environment, or the ancient strain? The Mindworm wondered as he strolled down the street. A girl passed him:

". . . oh but he's gonna be mad like last time wish I came right away so jealous kinda nice but he might bust me one some day be nice to him tonight there he is lam'post leaning on it looks kinda funny gawd I hope he ain't drunk looks kinda funny sleeping sick or bozhe moi gabblegabble-gabble . . ."

Her thoughts trailed into a foreign language of which the Mindworm knew not a word. After hysteria had gone she recalled, in the foreign language, that she had passed him.

The Mindworm, stimulated by the unfamiliar quality of the last feeding, determined to stay for some days. He checked in at a Main Street hotel.

Musing, he dragged his net:

". . . gobblegobblewhompyeargobblecheskygobblegabble-chyesh . . ."

". . . take him down cellar beat the can off the damn chesky thief put the fear of god into him teach him can't bust into no boxcars in *mah* parta the caounty . . ."

". . . gabblegabble . . ."

". . . phone ole Mister Ryan in She-cawgo and he'll tell them three-card monte grifters who got the horse-room rights in this necka the woods by damn don't pay protection money for no protection . . ."

The Mindworm followed that one further; it sounded as

though it could lead to some money if he wanted to stay in the town long enough.

The Eastern Europeans of the town, he mistakenly thought, were like the tramps and bums he had known and fed on during his years on the road—stupid and safe, safe and stupid, quite the same thing.

In the morning he found no mention of the square-headed boy's death in the town's paper and thought it had gone practically unnoticed. It had—by the paper, which was of, by and for the coal and iron company and its native-American bosses and straw bosses. The other town, the one without a charter or police force, with only an imported weekly newspaper or two from the nearest city, noticed it. The other town had roots more than two thousand years deep, which are hard to pull up. But the Mindworm didn't know it was there.

He fed again that night, on a giddy young streetwalker in her room. He had astounded and delighted her with a fistful of ten-dollar bills before he began to gorge. Again the delightful difference from city-bred folk was there. . . .

Again in the morning he had been unnoticed, he thought. The chartered town, unwilling to admit that there were streetwalkers or that they were found dead, wiped the slate clean; its only member who really cared was the native-American cop on the beat who had collected weekly from the dead girl.

The other town, unknown to the Mindworm, buzzed with it. A delegation went to the other town's only public officer. Unfortunately he was young, American-trained, perhaps even ignorant about some important things. For what he told them was: "My children, that is foolish superstition. Go home."

The Mindworm, through the day, roiled the surface of the town proper by allowing himself to be roped into a poker game in a parlor of the hotel. He wasn't good at it, he didn't like it, and he quit with relief when he had cleaned six shifty-eyed, hard-drinking loafers out of about three hundred dollars. One of them went straight to the police station and accused the unknown of being a sharper. A humorous sergeant, the Mindworm was pleased to note, joshed the loafer out of his temper.

Nightfall again, hunger again. . . .

He walked the streets of the town and found them empty. It was strange. The native-American citizens were out, tending bar, walking their beats, locking up their newspaper on the stones, collecting their rents, managing their movies—but where were the others? He cast his net:

". . . gobblegobblegobble whomp year gobble . . ."

". . . crazy old pollack mama of mine try to lock me in with Errol Flynn at the Majestic never know the difference if I sneak out the back . . ."

That was near. He crossed the street and it was nearer. He homed on the thought:

". . . jeez he's a hunka man like Stanley but he never looks at me that Vera Kowalik I'd like to kick her just once in the gobblegobblegobble crazy old mama won't be American so ashamed . . ."

It was half a block, no more, down a side street. Brick houses, two stories, with back yards on an alley. She was going out the back way.

How strangely quiet it was in the alley.

". . . ea-sy down them steps fix that damn board that's how she caught me last time what the hell are they all so scared of went to see Father Drugas won't talk bet somebody got it again that Vera Kowalik and her big . . ."

". . . gobble bozhe gobble whomp year gobble . . ."

She was closer; she was closer.

"All think I'm a kid show them who's a kid bet if Stanley caught me all alone out here in the alley dark and all he wouldn't think I was a kid that damn Vera Kowalik her folks don't think she's a kid . . ."

For all her bravado she was stark terrified when he said: "Hello."

"Who—who—who—?" she stammered.

Quick, before she screamed. Her terror was delightful.

Not too replete to be alert, he cast about, questing.

". . . gobblegobblegobble whomp year."

The countless eyes of the other town, with more than two thousand years of experience in such things, had been following him. What he had sensed as a meaningless hash of noise was actually an impassioned outburst in a nearby darkened house.

"Fools! fools! Now he has taken a virgin! I said not to wait. What will we say to her mother?"

An old man with handlebar mustache and, in spite of the heat, his shirt sleeves decently rolled down and buttoned at the cuffs, evenly replied: "My heart in me died with hers, Casimir, but one must be sure. It would be a terrible thing to make a mistake in such an affair."

The weight of conservative elder opinion was with him. Other old men with mustaches, some perhaps remembering mistakes long ago, nodded and said: "A terrible thing. A terrible thing."

The Mindworm strolled back to his hotel and napped on the made bed briefly. A tingle of danger awakened him. Instantly he cast out:

". . . gobblegobble whompyear."

". . . whampyir."

"WAMPYIR!"

Close! Close and deadly!

The door of his room burst open, and mustached old men with their shirt sleeves rolled down and decently buttoned at the cuffs unhesitatingly marched in, their thoughts a turmoil of alien noises, foreign gibberish that he could not wrap his mind around, disconcerting, from every direction.

The sharpened stake was through his heart and the scythe blade through his throat before he could realize that he had not been the first of his kind; and that what clever people have not yet learned, some quite ordinary people have not yet entirely forgotten.

The Rocket of 1955

THE scheme was all Fein's, but the trimmings that made it more than a pipe-dream, and its actual operation depended on me. How long the plan had been in incubation I do not know, but Fein, one spring day, broke it to me in crude form. I pointed out some errors, corrected and amplified on the thing in general, and told him that I'd have no part of it—and changed my mind when he threatened to reveal certain indiscretions committed by me some years ago.

It was necessary that I spend some months in Europe, conducting research work incidental to the scheme. I returned with recorded statements, old newspapers, and photostatic copies of certain documents. There was a brief, quiet interview with that old, bushy-haired Viennese worshiped incontinently by the mob; he was convinced by the evidence I had compiled that it would be wise to assist us.

You all know what happened next—it was the professor's historic radio broadcast. Fein had drafted the thing, I had rewritten it, and told the astronomer to assume a German accent while reading. Some of the phrases were beautiful: "American dominion over the very planets! . . . veil at last ripped aside . . . man defies gravity . . . travel through limitless space . . . plant the red-white-and-blue banner in the soil of Mars!"

The requested contributions poured in. Newspapers and magazines ostentatiously donated yard-long checks of a few thousand dollars; the government gave a welcome half-million; heavy sugar came from the "Rocket Contribution Week" held in the nation's public schools; but independent contributions were the largest. We cleared seven million dollars, and then started to build the spaceship.

The virginium that took up most of the money was tin-plate; the monoatomic fluorine that gave us our terrific speed was hydrogen. The take-off was a party for the newsreels: the big, gleaming bullet extravagant with vanes and projections; speeches by the professor; Farley, who was to fly it to Mars, grinning into the cameras. He climbed an outside ladder to the nose of the thing, then dropped into the steering compartment. I screwed down the sound-proof door, smiling as he hammered to be let out. To his surprise, there was no duplicate of the elaborate dummy controls he had been practicing on for the past few weeks.

I cautioned the pressmen to stand back under the shelter, and gave the professor the knife-switch that would send the rocket on its way. He hesitated too long—Fein hissed into his ear: "Anna Pareloff of Cracow, Herr Professor . . ."

The triple blade clicked into the sockets. The vaned projectile roared a hundred yards into the air with a wabbling curve—then exploded.

A photographer, eager for an angle-shot, was killed; so were some kids. The steel roof protected the rest of us. Fein and I shook hands, while the pressmen screamed into the telephones which we had provided.

But the professor got drunk, and, disgusted with the part he had played in the affair, told all and poisoned himself. Fein and I left the cash behind and hopped a freight. We were picked off it by a vigilance committee (headed by a man who had lost fifty cents in our rocket). Fein was too frightened to talk or write so they hanged him first, and gave me a paper and pencil to tell the story as best I could.

Here they come, with an insulting thick rope.

The Altar at Midnight

HE had quite a rum-blossom on him for a kid, I thought at first. But when he moved closer to the light by the cash register to ask the bartender for a match or something, I saw it wasn't that. Not just the nose. Broken veins on his cheeks, too, and the funny eyes. He must have seen me look, because he slid back away from the light.

The bartender shook my bottle of ale in front of me like a Swiss bell-ringer so it foamed inside the green glass.

"You ready for another, sir?" he asked.

I shook my head. Down the bar, he tried it on the kid—he was drinking scotch and water or something like that—and found out he could push him around. He sold him three scotch and waters in ten minutes.

When he tried for number four, the kid had his courage up and said, "I'll tell *you* when I'm ready for another, Jack." But there wasn't any trouble.

It was almost nine and the place began to fill up. The manager, a real hood type, stationed himself by the door to screen out the high-school kids and give the big hello to conventioneers. The girls came hurrying in, too, with their little makeup cases and their fancy hair piled up on them and their frozen faces with the perfect mouths drawn on them. One of them stopped to say something to the manager, some excuse about something, and he said: "That's aw ri'; getcha assina dressing room."

A three piece band behind the drapes at the back of the stage began to make warmup noises and there were two bartenders keeping busy. Mostly it was beer—a midweek crowd. I finished my ale and had to wait a couple of minutes before

43

I could get another bottle. The bar filled up from the end near the stage because all the customers wanted a good, close look at the strippers for their fifty-cent bottles of beer. But I noticed that nobody sat down next to the kid, or, if anybody did, he didn't stay long—you go out for some fun and the bartender pushes you around and nobody wants to sit next to you. I picked up my bottle and glass and went down on the stool to his left.

He turned to me right away and said: "What kind of a place is this, anyway?" The broken veins were all over his face, little ones, but so many, so close, that they made his face look something like marbled rubber. The funny look in his eyes was it—the trick contact lenses. But I tried not to stare and not to look away.

"It's okay," I said. "It's a good show if you don't mind a lot of noise from—"

He stuck a cigarette into his mouth and poked the pack at me. "I'm a spacer," he said, interrupting.

I took one of his cigarettes and said: "Oh."

He snapped a lighter for the cigarettes and said: "Venus."

I was noticing that his pack of cigarettes on the bar had some kind of yellow sticker instead of the blue tax stamp.

"Ain't that a crock?" he asked. "You can't smoke and they give you lighters for a souvenir. But it's a good lighter. On Mars last week, they gave us all some cheap pen-and-pencil sets."

"You get something every trip, hah?" I took a good, long drink of ale and he finished his scotch and water.

"Shoot. You call a trip a 'shoot'."

One of the girls was working her way down the bar. She was going to slide onto the empty stool at his right and give him the business, but she looked at him first and decided not to. She curled around me and asked if I'd buy her a li'l ole drink. I said no and she moved on to the next. I could kind of feel the young fellow quivering. When I looked at him, he stood up. I followed him out of the dump. The manager grinned without thinking and said, "G'night, boys," to us.

The kid stopped in the street and said to me: "You don't have to follow me around, Pappy." He sounded like one wrong word and I would get socked in the teeth.

"Take it easy. I know a place where they won't spit in your eye."

He pulled himself together and made a joke of it. "This I have to see," he said. "Near here?"

"A few blocks."

We started walking. It was a nice night.

"I don't know this city at all," he said. "I'm from Covington, Kentucky. You do your drinking at home there. We don't have places like this." He meant the whole Skid Row area.

"It's not so bad," I said. "I spend a lot of time here."

"Is that a fact? I mean, down home a man your age would likely have a wife and children."

"I do. The hell with them."

He laughed like a real youngster and I figured he couldn't even be twenty-five. He didn't have any trouble with the broken curbstones in spite of his scotch and waters. I asked him about it.

"Sense of balance," he said. "You have to be tops for balance to be a spacer—you spend so much time outside in a suit. People don't know how much. Punctures. And you aren't worth a damn if you lose your point."

"What's that mean?"

"Oh. Well, it's hard to describe. When you're outside and you lose your point, it means you're all mixed up, you don't know which way the can—that's the ship—which way the can is. It's having all that room around you. But if you have a good balance, you feel a little tugging to the ship, or maybe you just *know* which way the ship is without feeling it. Then you have your point and you can get the work done."

"There must be a lot that's hard to describe."

He thought that might be a crack and he clammed up on me.

"You call this Gandytown," I said after a while. "It's where the stove-up old railroad men hang out. This is the place."

It was the second week of the month, before everybody's pension check was all gone. Oswiak's was jumping. The Grandsons of the Pioneers were on the juke singing the *Man from Mars Yodel* and old Paddy Shea was jigging in the middle of the floor. He had a full seidel of beer in his right hand and his empty left sleeve was flapping.

The kid balked at the screen door. "Too damn bright," he said.

I shrugged and went on in and he followed. We sat down at

a table. At Oswiak's you can drink at the bar if you want to, but none of the regulars do.

Paddy jigged over and said: "Welcome home, Doc." He's a Liverpool Irishman; they talk like Scots, some say, but they sound like Brooklyn to me.

"Hello, Paddy. I brought somebody uglier than you. Now what do you say?"

Paddy jigged around the kid in a half-circle with his sleeve flapping and then flopped into a chair when the record stopped. He took a big drink from the seidel and said: "Can he do this?" Paddy stretched his face into an awful grin that showed his teeth. He has three of them. The kid laughed and asked me: "What the hell did you drag me into here for?"

"Paddy says he'll buy drinks for the house the day anybody uglier than he is comes in."

Oswiak's wife waddled over for the order and the kid asked us what we'd have. I figured I could start drinking, so it was three double scotches.

After the second round, Paddy started blowing about how they took his arm off without any anesthetics except a bottle of gin because the red-ball freight he was tangled up in couldn't wait.

That brought some of the other old gimps over to the table with their stories.

Blackie Bauer had been sitting in a boxcar with his legs sticking through the door when the train started with a jerk. Wham, the door closed. Everybody laughed at Blackie for being that dumb in the first place, and he got mad.

Sam Fireman has palsy. This week he was claiming he used to be a watchmaker before he began to shake. The week before, he'd said he was a brain surgeon. A woman I didn't know, a real old Boxcar Bertha, dragged herself over and began some kind of story about how her sister married a Greek, but she passed out before we found out what happened.

Somebody wanted to know what was wrong with the kid's face—Bauer, I think it was, after he came back to the table.

"Compression and decompression," the kid said. "You're all the time climbing into your suit and out of your suit. Inboard air's thin to start with. You get a few redlines—that's these ruptured blood vessels—and you say the hell with the money; all you'll make is just one more trip. But, God, it's a lot of money for anybody my age! You keep saying that until you can't be anything but a spacer. The eyes are hard-radiation scars."

"You like dot all ofer?" asked Oswiak's wife politely.

"All over, ma'am," the kid told her in a miserable voice. "But I'm going to quit before I get a Bowman Head."

I took a savage gulp at the raw Scotch.

"I don't care," said Maggie Rorty. "I think he's cute."

"Compared with—" Paddy began, but I kicked him under the table.

We sang for a while, and then we told gags and recited limericks for a while, and I noticed that the kid and Maggie had wandered into the back room—the one with the latch on the door.

Oswiak's wife asked me, very puzzled: "Doc, w'y dey do dot flyink by planyets?"

"It's the damn govermint," Sam Fireman said.

"Why not?" I said. "They got the Bowman Drive, why the hell shouldn't they use it? Serves 'em right." I had a double scotch and added: "Twenty years of it and they found out a few things they didn't know. Redlines are only one of them. Twenty years more, maybe they'll find out a few more things they didn't know. Maybe by the time there's a bathtub in every American home and an alcoholism clinic in every American town, they'll find out a whole *lot* of things they didn't know. And every American boy will be a pop-eyed, blood-raddled wreck, like our friend here, from riding the Bowman Drive."

"It's the damn govermint," Sam Fireman repeated.

"And what the hell did you mean by that remark about alcoholism?" Paddy said, real sore. "Personally, I can take it or leave it alone."

So we got to talking about that and everybody there turned out to be people who could take it or leave it alone.

It was maybe midnight when the kid showed at the table again, looking kind of dazed. I was drunker than I ought to be by midnight, so I said I was going for a walk. He tagged along and we wound up on a bench at Screwball Square. The soap-boxers were still going strong. As I said, it was a nice night. After a while, a pot-bellied old auntie who didn't give a damn about the face sat down and tried to talk the kid into going to see some etchings. The kid didn't get it and I led him over to hear the soap-boxers before there was trouble.

One of the orators was a mush-mouthed evangelist. "And

oh, my friends," he said, "when I looked through the porthole
of the spaceship and beheld the wonder of the Firmament—"

"You're a stinkin' Yankee liar!" the kid yelled at him. "You
say one damn more word about can-shootin' and I'll ram
your spaceship down your lyin' throat! Wheah's your redlines
if you're such a hot spacer?"

The crowd didn't know what he was talking about, but
"wheah's your redlines" sounded good to them, so they
heckled mushmouth off his box with it.

I got the kid to a bench. The liquor was working in him all
of a sudden. He simmered down after a while and asked:
"Doc, should I've given Miz Rorty some money? I asked her
afterward and she said she'd admire to have something to
remember me by, so I gave her my lighter. She seem' to be
real pleased with it. But I was wondering if maybe I embarrassed her by asking her right out. Like I tol' you, back
in Covington, Kentucky, we don't have places like that. Or
maybe we did and I just didn't know about them. But what do
you think I should've done about Miz Rorty?"

"Just what you did," I told him. "If they want money,
they ask you for it first. Where you staying?"

"Y. M. C. A.," he said, almost asleep. "Back in Covington,
Kentucky, I was a member of the Y and I kept up my mem-
bership. They have to let me in because I'm a member.
Spacers have all kinds of trouble, Doc. Woman trouble. Hotel
trouble. Fam'ly trouble. Religious trouble. I was raised a
Southern Baptist, but wheah's Heaven, anyway? I ask' Doctor
Chitwood las' time home before the redlines got so thick—
Doc, you aren't a minister of the Gospel, are you? I hope I
di'n' say anything to offend you."

"No offense, son," I said. "No offense."

I walked him to the avenue and waited for a fleet cab. It
was almost five minutes. The independent cabs roll drunks
and dent the fenders of fleet cabs if they show up in Skid
Row and then the fleet drivers have to make reports on their
own time to the company. It keeps them away. But I got one
and dumped the kid in.

"The Y Hotel," I told the driver. "Here's five. Help him in
when you get there."

When I walked through Screwball Square again, some college kids were yelling "wheah's your redlines" at old Charlie,
the last of the Wobblies.

Old Charlie kept roaring: "The hell with your breadlines! I'm talking about atomic bombs. *Right—up—there!*" And he pointed at the Moon.

It was a nice night, but the liquor was dying in me.

There was a joint around the corner, so I went in and had a drink to carry me to the club; I had a bottle there. I got into the first cab that came.

"Athletic Club," I said.

"Inna dawghouse, harh?" the driver said, and he gave me a big personality smile.

I didn't say anything and he started the car.

He was right, of course. I was in everybody's doghouse. Some day I'd scare hell out of Tom and Lise by going home and showing them what their daddy looked like.

Down at the Institute, I was in the doghouse.

"Oh, dear," everybody at the Institute said to everybody, "I'm sure I don't know what ails the man. A lovely wife and two lovely grown children and she had to tell him 'either you go or I go.' And *drinking!* And this is rather subtle, but it's a well-known fact that neurotics seek out low company to compensate for their guilt-feelings. The *places* he frequents. Doctor Francis Bowman, the man who made space-flight a reality. The man who put the Bomb Base on the Moon! Really, I'm sure I don't know what ails him."

The hell with them all.

Thirteen O'Clock

I

PETER PACKER folded the carpenter's rule and rose from his knees, brushing dust from the neat crease of his serge trousers. No doubt of it—the house had a secret attic room. Peter didn't know anything about sliding panels or hidden buttons; in the most direct way imaginable he lifted the axe he had brought and crunched it into the wall.

On his third blow he holed through. The rush of air from the darkness was cool and sweet. Smart old boy, his grandfather, thought Peter. Direct ventilation all over the house—even in a false compartment. He chopped away heartily, the hollow strokes ringing through the empty attic and down the stairs.

He could have walked through the hole erect when he was satisfied with his labors; instead he cautiously turned a flashlight inside the space. The beam was invisible; all dust had long since settled. Peter grunted. The floor seemed to be sound. He tested it with one foot, half in, half out of the hidden chamber. It held.

The young man stepped through easily, turning the flash on walls and floor. The room was not large, but it was cluttered with a miscellany of objects—chests, furniture, knick-knacks and what-nots. Peter opened a chest, wondering about pirate gold. But there was no gold, for the thing was full to the lid with chiffons in delicate hues. A faint fragrance of musk filled the air; sachets long since packed away were not entirely gone.

Funny thing to hide away, thought Peter. But Grandfather Packer had been a funny man—having this house built to his own very sound plans, waiting always on the Braintree docks for the China and India Clippers and what rare cargo they might have brought. Chiffons! Peter pocked around in the box for a moment, then closed the lid again. There were others.

He turned the beam of the light on a wall lined with shelves. Pots of old workmanship—spices and preserves, probably. And a clock. Peter stared at the clock. It was about two by two by three feet—an unusual and awkward size. The workmanship was plain, the case of crudely finished wood. And yet there was something about it—his eyes widened as he realized what it was. The dial showed thirteen hours!

Between the flat figures XII and I there was another—an equally flat XIII. What sort of freak this was the young man did not know. Vaguely he conjectured on prayer-time, egg-boiling and all the other practical applications of chronometry. But nothing he could dredge up from his well-stored mind would square with this freak. He set the flash on a shelf and hefted the clock in his arms, lifting it easily.

This, he thought, would bear looking into. Putting the light in his pocket he carried the clock down the stairs to his second-floor bedroom. It looked strangely incongruous there, set on a draftsman's table hung with rules and T squares. Determinedly Peter was beginning to pry open the back with a chisel, when it glided smoothly open without tooling. There was better construction in the old timeplace than he had realized. The little hinges were still firm and in working order. He peered into the works and ticked his nail against one of the chimes. It sounded sweet and clear. The young man took a pair of pliers. Lord knew where the key was, he thought, as he began to wind the clock. He nudged the pendulum. Slowly it got under way, ticking loudly. The thing had stopped at 12:59. That would be nearly one o'clock in any other timepiece; on this the minute hand crept slowly toward the enigmatic XIII.

Peter wound the striking mechanism carefully, and watched as a little whir sounded. The minute hand met the Roman numeral, and with a click the chimes sounded out in an eerie, jangling discord. Peter thought with sudden confusion that all was not well with the clock as he had thought. The chimes grew louder, filling the little bedroom with their clang.

Horrified, the young man put his hands on the clock as though he could stop off the noise. As he shook the old cabinet the peals redoubled until they battered against the ear-

drums of the draftsman, ringing in his skull and resounding
from the walls, making instruments dance and rattle on the
drawing-board. Peter drew back, his hands to his ears. He was
filled with nausea, his eyes bleared and smarting. As the
terrible clock thundered out its din without end he reached
the door feebly, the room swaying and spinning about him,
nothing real but the suddenly glowing clock-dial and the
clang and thunder of its chimes.

He opened the door and it ceased; he closed his eyes in
relief as his nausea passed. He looked up again, and his eyes
widened with horror. Though it was noon outside a night-
wind fanned his face, and though he was on the second-story
landing of his Grandfather Packer's house dark trees rose
about him, stretching as far as the eye could see.

For three hours—by his wristwatch's luminous dial—Peter
had wandered, aimless and horrified, waiting for dawn. The
aura of strangeness that hung over the forest in which he
walked was bearable; it was the gnawing suspicion that he had
gone mad that shook him to his very bones. The trees were no
ordinary things, of that he was sure. For he had sat down
under one forest giant and leaned back against its bole only to
rise with a cry of terror. He had felt its pulse beat slowly and
regularly under the bark. After that he did not dare to rest,
but he was a young and normal male. Whether he would or
not he found himself blundering into ditches and stones from
sheer exhaustion. Finally, sprawled on the ground, he slept.

Peter woke stiff and sore from his nap on the bare ground,
but he felt better for it. The sun was high in the heavens; he
saw that it was about eleven o'clock. Remembering his terrors
of the night he nearly laughed at himself. This was a forest,
and there were any number of sane explanations how he got
here. An attack of amnesia lasting about twelve hours would
be one cause. And there were probably others less disturbing.

He thought the country might be Maine. God knew how
many trains or busses he had taken since he lost his memory
in his bedroom. Beginning to whistle he strode through the
woods. Things were different in the daytime.

There was a sign ahead! He sprinted up to its base. The
thing was curiously large, painted in red characters on a great
slab of wood, posted on a dead tree some twelve feet from the
ground. The sign said ELLIL. He rolled the name over in his

mind and decided that he didn't recognize it. But he couldn't be far from a town or house.

Ahead of him sounded a thunderous grunt.

"Bears!" he thought in a panic. (They had been his childhood bogies.) But it was no bear, he saw. He almost wished it was. For the thing that was veering on him was a frightful composite of every monster of mythology, menacing him with sabre-like claws and teeth and gusts of flame from its ravening throat. It stood only about as high as the man, and its legs were long, but it seemed ideally styled for destruction.

Without ado he jumped for a tree and dug his toes into the grooves of the bark, shinning up it like a child. With the creature's flaming breath scorching his heels he climbed, stopping only at the third set of main branches, twenty-five feet from the ground. There he clung, limp and shuddering, and looked down.

The creature was hopping grotesquely about the base of the tree, its baleful eyes on him. The man's hand reached for a firmer purchase on the branch, and part came away in his hand. He had picked a sort of coconut—heavy, hard, and with sharp corners. Peter raised his eyes. Why not? Carefully noting the path that the creature below took around the trunk he poised the fruit carefully. Wetting a finger, he adjusted the placing. On a free drop that long you had to allow for windage, he thought.

Twice more around went the creature, and then its head and the murderous fruit reached the same point at the same time. There was a crunching noise which Peter could hear from where he was and the insides of its head spilled on the forest sward.

"Clever," said a voice beside him on the branch.

He turned with a cry. The speaker was only faintly visible— the diaphanous shadow of a young girl, not more than eighteen, he thought. Calmly it went on, "You must be very mancic to be able to land a fruit so accurately. Did he give you an extra sense?" Her tone was light, but from what he could see of her dim features they were curled in an angry smile.

Nearly letting go of the branch in his bewilderment he answered as calmly as he could, "I don't know who you mean. And what is mancic?"

"Innocent," she said coldly. "Eh? I could push you off this

branch without a second thought. But first you tell me where Almarish got the model for you. I might turn out a few myself. Are you a doppleganger or a golem?"

—"Neither," he spat, bewildered and horrified. "I don't even know what they are!"

"Strange," said the girl. "I can't read you." Her eyes squinted prettily and suddenly became solid, luminous wedges in her transparent face. "Well," she sighed, "let's get out of this." She took the man by his elbow and dropped from the branch, hauling him after her. Ready for a sickening impact with the ground, Peter winced as his heels touched it light as a feather. He tried to disengage the girl's grip, but it was steel-hard.

"None of that," she warned him. "I have a blast-finger. Or didn't he tell you?"

"What's a blast-finger?" demanded the engineer.

"Just so you won't try anything," she commented. "Watch." Her body solidified then, and she pointed her left index finger at a middling-sized tree. Peter hardly saw what happened, being more interested in the incidental miracle of her face and figure. But his attention was distracted by a flat crash of thunder and sudden glare. And the tree was riven as if by a terrific stroke of lightning. Peter smelled ozone as he looked from the tree to the girl's finger and back again. "Okay," he said.

"No nonsense?" she asked. "Come on."

They passed between two trees, and the vista of forest shimmered and tore, revealing a sort of palace—all white stone and maple timbers. "That's my place," said the girl.

II

"Now," she said, settling herself into a cane-backed chair. Peter looked about the room. It was furnished comfortably with pieces of antique merit, in the best New England tradition. His gaze shifted to the girl, slender and palely luminous, with a half-smile playing about her chisled features.

"Do you mind," he said slowly, "not interrupting until I'm finished with what I have to say?"

"A message from Almarish? Go on."

And at that he completely lost his temper. "Listen, you snip!" he raged. "I don't know who you are or where I am but I'd like to tell you that this mystery isn't funny or even mysterious—just downright rude. Do you get that? Now—my name is Peter Packer. I live in Braintree, Mass. I make my living as a consulting engineer. This place obviously isn't Braintree, Mass. Right? Then where is it?"

"Ellil," said the girl simply.

"I saw that on a sign," said Packer. "It still doesn't mean anything to me. Where is Ellil?"

Her face became suddenly grave. "You may be telling the truth," she said thoughtfully. "I do not know yet. Will you allow me to test you?"

"Why should I?"

"Remember my blast-finger?"

Packer winced. "Yes," he said. "What are the tests?"

"The usual," she smiled. "Rosemary and garlic, crucifixes and the secret name of Jehovah. If you get through those you're okay."

"Then get on with it," he said, confusedly.

"Hold these." She passed him a flowery sprig and a clove of garlic. He took them, one in each hand. "All right?" he asked.

"On those, yes. Now take the cross and read this name. You can put the vegetables down now."

He followed instructions, stammering over the harsh Hebrew word. In a cold fury the girl sprang to her feet and leveled her left index finger at him. "Clever," she blazed. "But you can't get away with it! I'll blow you so wide open—"

"Wait," he pleaded. "What did I do?" The girl, though sweet-looking, seemed to be absolutely irresponsible.

"Mispronounced the Name," she snapped. "Because you can't say it straight without crumbling into dust!"

He looked at the paper again and read aloud slowly and carefully. "Was that right?" he asked.

Crestfallen, the girl sat down. "Yes," she said. "I'm sorry. You seem to be okay. A real human. Now what do you want to know?"

"Well—who are you?"

"My name's Melicent." She smiled deprecatingly. "I'm a sorceress."

"I can believe that. Now why should you take me for a demon, or whatever you thought I was?"

"Doppleganger," she corrected him. "I was sure—well, I'd better begin at the beginning.

"You see, I haven't been a sorceress very long—only two years. My mother was a witch—a real one, and first-class. All I know I learned from her—never studied it formally. My mother didn't die a natural death, you see. Almarish got her."

"Who's Almarish?"

She wrinkled her mouth with disgust. "A thug!" she spat. "He and his gang of half-breed demons are out to get control of Ellil. My mother wouldn't stand for it—she told him right out flat over a Multiplex Apparition. And after that he was gunning for her steady—no letup at all. And believe me, there are mighty few witches who can stand up under much of that, but Mother stood him off for fifteen years. They got my father —he wasn't much good—a little while after I was born. Vampires.

"Mother got caught alone in the woods one morning without her tools—unguents, staffs and things—by a whole flock of golems and zombies." The girl shuddered. "Some of them —well, Mother finished about half before they overwhelmed her and got a stake of myrtle through her heart. That finished her—she lost all her magic, of course, and Almarish sent a plague of ants against her. Adding insult to injury!" There were real tears of rage in her eyes.

"And what's this Almarish doing now?" Peter was fascinated.

Melicent shrugged. "He's after me," she said simply. "The bandur you killed was one of my watchdogs. And I thought he'd sent you. I'm sorry."

"I see," he breathed slowly. "What powers has he?"

"The usual, I suppose. But he has no principles about using them. And he has his gang—I can't afford real retainers. Of course I whip up some simulacra whenever I hold a reception or anything of that sort. Just images to serve and take wraps. They can't fight."

Peter tightened his jaw. "You must be in a bad way."

The girl looked him full in the eye, her lip trembling. She choked out, "I'm in such a hell of a spot!" and then the gates opened and she was weeping as if her heart would break. He frozenly, wondering how he could comfort a despondent sorceress. "There, there," he said tentatively.

She wiped her eyes and looked at him. "I'm sorry," she said sniffing. "But it's seeing a friendly face again after all these years—no callers but leprechauns and things. You don't know what it's like."

"I wonder," said Peter, "how you'd like to live in Braintree."

"I don't know," she said brightly. "But how could I get there?"

"There should be at least one way."

"But why—what was that?" shot out the girl, snatching up a wand.

"Knock on the door," said Peter. "Shall I open it?"

"Please," said Melicent nervously, holding up the slender staff. He stood aside and swung the door wide. In walked a curious person of mottled red and white coloring. One eye was small and blue, the other large and savagely red. His teeth were quite normal—except that the four canines protruded two inches each out of his mouth. He walked with a limp; one shoe seemed curiously small. And there was a sort of bulge in the trousers that he wore beneath his formal morning-coat.

"May I introduce myself," said the individual, removing his sleek black topper. "I am Balthazar Pike. You must be Miss Melicent? And this—ah—zombie?" He indicated Peter with a leer.

"Mr. Packer, Mr. Pike," said the girl. Peter stared in horror while the creature murmured, "Enchanted."

Melicent drew herself up proudly. "And this, I suppose," she said, "is the end?"

"I fear so, Miss Melicent," said the creature regretfully. "I have my orders. Your house has been surrounded by picked forces; any attempt to use your blast-finger or any other weapon of offense will be construed as resistance. Under the laws of civilized warfare we are empowered to reduce you to ashes should such resistance be forthcoming. May I have your reply?"

The girl surveyed him haughtily, then, with a lighting-like sweep of her wand, seemed to blot out every light in the room. Peter heard her agitated voice, "We're in a neutral screen, Mr. Packer. I won't be able to keep it up for long. Listen! That was one of Almarish's stinkers—big cheese. He didn't expect any trouble from me. He'll take me captive as soon as they break the screen down. Do you want to help me?"

"Of course!"

"Good. Then you find the third oak from the front door on the left and walk widdershins three times. You'll find out what to do from them."

"Walk how?" asked Peter.

"Widdershins—counterclockwise. Lord, you're dumb!"

Then the lights seemed to go on again, and Peter saw that the room was filled with the half-breed creatures. With an expression of injured dignity the formally-attired Balthazar Pike asked, "Are you ready to leave now, Miss Melicent? Quite ready?"

"Thank you, General, yes," said the girl coldly. Two of the creatures took her arms and walked her from the room. Peter saw that as they stepped over the threshold they vanished, all three. The last to leave was Pike, who turned and said to the man: "I must remind you, Mister—er—ah—that you are trespassing. This property now belongs to the Almarish Realty Corporation. All offenders will be prosecuted to the fullest extent of the law. Good day, Mister—er—ah—". With which he stepped over the door and vanished.

Hastily Peter followed him across the line, but found himself alone outside the house. For which he was grateful. "Third oak from the left door," he repeated. Simple enough. Feeling foolish he walked widdershins three times around and stopped dead waiting for something.

What a sweet, brave kid she had been! He hoped nothing would really happen to her—before he got there.

He felt a sort of tugging at his serge trousers and stepped back in alarm. "Well?" shrilled a small voice. Peter looked down and winced. The dirtiest, most bedraggled little creature he had ever seen was regarding him with tiny, sharp eyes. There were others, too, squatting on pebbles and toadstools.

"Miss Melicent told me to ask you what I should do," said Peter. As the little leader of the troop glared at him he added hastily, "If you please."

"Likely tale," piped the voice of the creature. "What's in it for us?"

"I dunno," he said bewildered. "What do you want?"

"Green cloth," the creature answered promptly. "Lots of it. And if you have any small brass buttons, them too."

Peter hastily conducted on inventory of his person. "I'm sorry," he said hesitantly. "I haven't any green. How about blue? I can spare my vest." He carefully lowered the garment to the ground among the little people.

"Looks all right," said the leader. "Jake!" One of the creatures advanced and fingered the cloth. "Hmm—" he said. "Good material." Then there was a whispered consultation with the leader, who at last shouted up to Peter: "Head East for water. You can't miss it!"

"Hey," said Peter, blinking. But they were already gone. And though he widdershin-walked for the next half hour and even tried a few incantations remembered from his childhood they did not come back, nor did his vest.

So, with his back to the sinking sun, he headed East for water.

III

"Mahoora City Limits," said the sign. Peter scratched his head and passed it. He had hit the stretch of highway a few miles back once he had got out of the forest, and it seemed to be leading straight into a city of some kind. There was a glow ahead in the sky; a glow which abruptly became a glare.

Peter gasped. "Buildings—skyscrapers!" Before him reared a sort of triple Wall Street with which were combined the most spectacular features of Rockefeller Center. In the sudden way in which things happened in Ellil he turned a blind corner in the road and found himself in the thick of it.

A taxi roared past him; with a muttered imprecation he jumped out of the way. The bustling people on the sidewalks ignored him completely. It was about six o'clock; they were probably going home from their offices. They were all sorts of people—women and girls, plain and pretty, men and boys, slim, fat, healthy and dissipated. And striding along in lordly indifference Peter saw a cop.

"Excuse me," said Peter elbowing his way through the crowd

to the member of Mahoora's finest. "Can you tell me where I can find water?" That was, he realized, putting it a bit crudely. But he was hopelessly confused by the traffic and swarms of pedestrians.

The cop turned on him with a glassy stare. "Water?" he rumbled. "Would yez be wantin' tap, ditch, fire—or cologne?" Peter hesitated. He didn't know, he realized in a sudden panic. The elves, or whatever they had been, hadn't specified. Cagily he raised his hand to his brow and muttered, " 'Scuse me— previous engagement—made the appointment for today— just forgot—" He was edging away from the cop when he felt a hand on his arm.

"What was that about water?" asked the cop hoarsely, putting his face near Peter's. Desperately Peter blurted: "The water I have to find to lick Almarish!" Who could tell? Maybe the cop would help him.

"What?" thundered M.P.D. Shield No. 2435957607. "And me a loyal supporter of the Mayor Almarish Freedom Peace and Progress Reform Administration?" He frowned. "You look subversive to me—come on!" He raised his nightstick suggestively, and Peter meekly followed him through the crowds.

"How'd they get you in here?" asked Peter's cell-mate.

Peter inspected him. He was a short, dark sort of person with a pair of disconcertingly bright eyes. "Suspicion," said Peter evasively. "How about you?"

"Practicing mancy without a license, theoretically. Actually because I tried to buck the Almarish machine. You know how it is?"

"Can't say I do," answered Peter. "I'm a stranger here."

"Yeah? Well—like this. Few years ago we had a neat little hamlet here. Mahoora was the biggest little city in these parts of Ellil, though I say it myself. A little industry—magic chalices for export, sandals of swiftness, invisibility cloaks, invincible weapons—you know?"

"Um," said Peter noncommittally.

"Well, I had a factory—modest little chemical works. We turned out love-philtres from my own prescription. It's what I call a neat dodge—eliminates the *balneum mariae* entirely from the processing, cuts down drying time—maybe you aren't familiar with the latest things in the line?"

"Sorry, no."

"Oh. Well, then, in came those plugs of Almarish. Flying goonsquads that wrecked plants and shops on order; spies, provocateurs, everything. Soon they'd run out every racketeer in the place and hi-jacked them lock stock and barrel. Then they went into politics. There was a little scandal about buying votes with fairy gold—people kicked when it turned into ashes. But they smoothed that over when they got in.

"And then—! Graft right and left, patronage, unemployment, rotten food scandals, bribery, inefficiency—everything that's on the list. And this is their fifth term. How do you like that?"

"Lord," said Peter, shocked. "But how do they stay in office?"

"Oh," grinned his friend. "The first thing they did was to run up some imposing public works—tall buildings, bridges, highways and monuments. Then they let it out that they were partly made of half-stuff. You know what that is?"

"No," said Peter. "What is it?"

"Well—it's a little hard to describe. But it isn't really there and it isn't really not there. You can walk on it and pick it up and things, but—well, it's a little hard to describe. The kicker is this. Half-stuff is there only as long as you—the one who prepared a batch of it that is—keep the formula going. So if we voted those leeches out of office they'd relax their formula and the half-stuff would vanish and the rest of the buildings and bridges and highways and monuments would fall with a helluva noise and damage. How do you like that?"

"Efficiency plus," said Peter. "Where's this Almarish hang out?"

"The mayor?" asked his cell-mate sourly. "You don't think he'd be seen in the city, do you? Some disgruntled citizen might sic a flock of vampires on his honor. He was elected in absentia. I hear he lives around Mal-Tava way."

"Where's that?" asked Peter eagerly.

"You don't know? Say, you're as green as they come! That's a pretty nasty corner of Ellil—the nastiest anywhere, I guess. It's a volcania region, and those lava-nymphs are tough molls. Then there's a dragon-ranch around there. The owner got careless and showed up missing one day. The dragons broke out and ran wild. Anything else?"

"No," said Peter, heavy-hearted. "I guess not."

"That's good. Because I think we're going to trial right

now." A guard was opening the door, club poised. "His honor, Judge Balthazar Pike will see you now," said the warden. Peter groaned.

The half-breed demon, his sartorial splendor of the preceding afternoon replaced by judiciary black silk, smiled grimly on the two prisoners. "Mr. Morden," he said indicating the erstwhile manufacturer, "and Mr.—er—ah?"

"Packer!" Peter shouted. "What are you doing here?"

"Haw!" laughed the judge. "That's what I was going to ask you. But first we have this matter of Mr. Morden to dispose of. Excuse me a moment? Clerk, read the charges."

A cowed-looking little man picked an index-card from a stack and read: "Whereas Mr. Percival Morden of Mahoora has been apprehended in the act of practicing mancy and whereas this Mr. Morden does not possess an approved license for such practice it is directed that His Honor Chief Judge Balthazar Pike declare him guilty of the practice of mancy without a license. Signed, Mayor Almarish. Vote straight Peace and Progress Reform Party for a clean and efficient administration." He paused for a moment and looked timidly at the judge who was cleaning his talons. "That's it, your honor," he said.

"Oh—thank you. Now Morden—guilty or not guilty?"

"What's the difference?" asked the manufacturer sourly. "Not guilty, I guess."

"Thank you." The judge took a coin from his pocket. "Heads or tails?" he asked.

"Tails," answered Morden. Then, aside to Peter, "It's magic, of course. You can't win." The half-breed demon spun the coin dexterously on the judical bench; it wobbled, slowed, and fell with a tinkle. The judge glanced at it. "Sorry, old man," he said sympathetically. "You seem to be guilty. Imprisonment for life in an oak-tree. You'll find Merlin de Bleys in there with you, I rather fancy. You'll like him. Next case," he called sharply as Morden fell through a trapdoor in the floor.

Peter advanced before the bar of justice. "Can't we reason this thing out?" he asked hopelessly. "I mean, I'm a stranger here and if I've done anything I'm sorry—"

"Tut!" exclaimed the demon. He had torn the cuticle of his left index talon, and it was bleeding. He stanched the green liquid with a handkerchief and looked down at the man.

"Done anything?" he asked mildly. "Oh—dear me, no! Except for a few trifles like felonious impediment of an officer in the course of his duty, indecent display, seditious publication, high treason and unlawful possession of military and naval secrets—done anything?" His two odd eyes looked reproachfully down on the man.

Peter felt something flimsy in his hand. Covertly he looked and saw a slip of blue paper on which was written in green ink: "This is Hugo, my other watchdog. Feed him once a day on green vegetables. He does not like tobacco. In haste, Melicent."

There was a stir in the back of the courtroom, and Peter turned to see one of the fire-breathing horrors which had first attacked him in the forest tearing down the aisle lashing out to right and left, incinerating a troop of officers with one blast of its terrible breath. Balthazar Pike was crawling around under his desk, bawling for more police.

Peter cried, "You can add one more—possession of a bandur without a license! Sic 'em, Hugo!" The monster flashed an affectionate look at him and went on with the good work of clearing the court. The man sprang aside as the trapdoor opened beneath his feet and whirled on a cop who was trying to swarm over him. With a quick one-two he laid him out and proceeded to the rear of the courtroom, where Hugo was standing off a section of the fire-department that was trying to extinguish his throat. Peter snatched an axe from one and mowed away heartily. Resistance melted away in a hurry, and Peter pushed the hair out of his eyes to find that they were alone in the court.

"Come on, boy," he said. Whistling cheerily he left the building, the bandur at his heels, smoking gently. Peter collared a cop—the same one who had first arrested him. "Now," he snarled. "Where do I find water?"

Stuttering with fright, and with two popping eyes on the bandur, the officer said, "The harbor's two blocks down the street if you mean—"

"Never mind what I mean!" Luxuriating in his new-found power Peter strode off pugnaciously, Hugo following.

IV

"I beg your pardon—are you looking for water?" asked a tall, dark man over Peter's shoulder. Hugo growled and let loose a tongue of flame at the stranger's foot. "Shuddup, Hugo," said Peter. Then, turning to the stranger, "As a matter of fact I was. Do you—?"

"I heard about you from them," said the stranger. "You know. The little people."

"Yes," said Peter. "What do I do now?"

"Underground Railroad," said the stranger. "Built after the best Civil War model. Neat, speedy and efficient. Transportation at half the usual cost. I hope you weren't planning to go by magic carpet?"

"No," Peter assured him hastily. "I never use them."

"That's great," said the stranger swishing his long black cloak. "Those carpet people—stifling industry. They spread a whispering campaign that our road was unsafe! Can you imagine it?"

"Unsafe," scoffed Peter. "I'll bet they wish their carpets were half as safe as your railroad!"

"Well," said the stranger thoughtfully, "perhaps not half as safe . . . No; I wouldn't say half as safe . . ." He seemed likely to go on indefinitely; Peter asked, "Where do I get the Underground?"

"A little East of here," said the stranger. He looked about apprehensively. "We'd better not be seen together," he muttered out of the corner of his mouth. "Meet you over there by the clock-tower—you can get it there."

"Okay," said Peter. "But why the secrecy?"

"We're really underground," said the stranger, walking away.

Peter rejoined him at the corner of the clock-tower; with an elaborate display of unconcern the stranger walked off, Peter following at some distance. Soon they were again in the forest that seemed to border the city of Mahoora. Once they were past the city-limits sign the stranger turned, smiling.

"I guess we're safe now," he said. "They could try a raid and drag us back across the line, but they wouldn't like to play with your bandur. Here's the station."

He pressed a section of bark on a huge tree; silently it slid open like a door. Peter saw a row of steps leading down into blackness. "Sort of spooky," he said.

"Not at all! I have the place ghostproofed once a year." The stranger led the way, taking out what looked like a five-branched electric torch. "What's that?" asked Peter, fascinated by the weird blue light it shed.

"Hand of glory," said the stranger casually. Peter looked closer and shuddered, holding his stomach. Magic, he thought, was all right up to the point where it became grave-robbery.

They arrived at a neatly tiled station; Peter was surprised to find that the trains were tiny things. The one pulled up on the tracks was not as high as he was. "You'll have to stoke, of course," said the stranger.

"What?" demanded Peter indignantly.

"Usual arrangement. Are you coming or aren't you?"

"Of course—but it seems strange," complained Peter climbing into the engine. Hugo climbed up into the coal car and curled up emitting short smoky bursts of flame which caused the stranger to keep glancing at him in fear for his fuel.

"What's in the rest of the train?" asked Peter.

"Freight. This is the through cannonball to Mal-Tava. I have a special shipment for Almarish. Books and things, furniture, a few cases of liquor—you know?"

"Yes. Any other passengers?"

"Not this month. I haven't much trouble with them. They're usually knights and things out to kill sorcerers like Almarish. They take their horses along or send them ahead by carpet. Do you plan to kill Almarish?"

Peter choked. "Yes," he finally said. "What's it to you?"

"Nothing—I take your money and leave you where you want to go. A tradesman can't afford opinions. Let's get up some steam, eh?"

Amateurishly Peter shoveled coal into the little furnace while the stranger in the black cloak juggled with steam-valves and levers. "Don't be worried," he advised Peter. "You'll get the hang of things after a while." He glanced at a watch. "Here we go," he said, yanking the whistle-cord.

The train started off into its tunnel, sliding smoothly and almost silently along, the only noise being from the driving rods. "Why doesn't it clack against the rails?" asked Peter.

"Levitation. Didn't you notice? We're an inch off the track. Simple, really."

"Then why have a track?" asked Peter.

The stranger smiled and said, "Without—" then stopped abruptly and looked concerned and baffled. And that was all the answer Peter got.

"Wake up," shouted the stranger nudging Peter. "We're in the war zone!"

"Zasso?" asked Peter, blinking. He had been napping after hours of steady travel. "What war zone?"

"Trolls—*you* know."

"No, I don't!" snapped Peter. "What side are we on?"

"Depends on who stops us," said the stranger, speeding the engine. They were out of the tunnel now, Peter saw, speeding along a couple of inches above the floor of an immense dim cave. Ahead the glittering double strand of the track stretched into the distance.

"Oh—oh!" muttered the cloaked stranger. "Trouble ahead!" Peter saw a vague, stirring crowd before them. "Those trolls?" he asked.

"Yep," answered the engineer resignedly, slowing the train. "What do you want?" he asked a solid looking little man in a ragged uniform. "To get the hell out of here," said the little man. He was about three feet tall, Peter saw. "What happened?" he asked.

"The lousy Insurgents licked us," said the troll. "Will you let us on the train before they cut us down?"

"First," said the engineer methodically, "there isn't room. Second, I have to keep friends with the party in power. Third, you know very well that you can't be killed."

"What if we are immortal?" asked the troll. "Would you like to live forever scattered in little pieces?"

"Second," said Peter abruptly, "you get out of it as best you can." He was speaking to the engineer. "And first, you can dump all the freight you have for Almarish. He won't want it anyway when I'm through with him."

"That right?" asked the troll.

"Not by me!" exploded the engineer. "Now get your gang off the track before I plough them under!"

"Hugo," whispered Peter. With a lazy growl the bandur scorched the nape of the engineer's head.

"All right," said the engineer. "All right. Use force—all right." Then, to the leader of the trolls, "You tell your men they can unload the freight and get as comfortable as they can."

"Wait!" said Peter. "Inasmuch as I got you out of this scrape—I think—would you be willing to help me out in a little affair of honor with Almarish?"

"Sure!" said the troll. "Anything at all. You know, for a surface-dweller you're not half bad!" With which he began to spread the good news among his army.

Later, when they were all together in the cab, taking turns with the shovel, the troll introduced himself as General Skaldberg of the Third Loyalist Army.

Speeding ahead again at full speed the end of the cavern was in sight when another swarm of trolls blocked the path. "Go through them!" ordered Peter coldly.

"For pity's sake," pleaded the stranger. "Think of what this will do to my franchise!"

"That's your worry," said the General. "You fix it up with the Insurgents. *We* gave you the franchise anyway—they have no right of search."

"Maybe," muttered the engineer. He closed his eyes as they went slapping into the band of trolls under full steam. When it was all over and they were again tearing through the tunnel he looked up. "How many?" he asked brokenly.

"Only three," said the general regretfully. "Why didn't you do a good job while you were at it?"

"You should have had your men fire from the freight-cars," said the engineer coldly.

"Too bad I didn't think of it. Could you turn back and take them in a surprise attack?"

The engineer cursed violently, giving no direct answer. But for the next half hour he muttered to himself distraitly, groaning "Franchise!" over and over again.

"How much farther before we get to Mal-Tava?" asked Peter glumly.

"Very soon now," said the troll. "I was there once. Very broken terrain—fine for guerilla work."

"Got any ideas on how to handle the business of Almarish?"

The general scratched his head. "As I remember it," he said slowly, "it's a funny tactical problem—practically no fortifications within the citadel—everything lumped outside in a wall

of steel. Of course Almarish probably has a lot on the ball
personally. All kinds of direct magic at his fingertips. And
that's where I get off with my men. We trolls don't even pré-
tend to know the fine points of thaumaturgy. Mostly straight
military stuff with us."

"So I have to face him alone?"

"More or less," said the general. "I have a couple of guys
that majored in Military Divination at Ellil Tech Prep. They
can probably give you a complete layout of the citadel, but
they won't be responsible for illusions, multiplex apparitions or
anything else Almarish might decide to throw in the way.
My personal advice to you is—be sceptical."

"Yes?" asked Peter miserably.

"Exactly," said Skaldberg. "The real difficulty in handling
arcane warfare is in knowing what's there and what ain't.
Have you any way of sneaking in a confederate? Not a spy,
exactly—we military men don't approve of spying—but a sort
of—ah—one-man intelligence unit."

"I have already," said Peter diffidently. "She's a sorceress,
but not much good I think. Has a blast-finger, though."

"Very good," grunted Skaldberg. "Very good indeed. How
we could have used her against the Insurgents! The hounds
had us in a sort of peninsular spot—with only one weak line
of supply and communication between us and the main force
—and I was holding a hill against a grand piquet of flying
carpets that were hurling thunderbolts at our munitions supply. But their sights were away off and they only got a few
of our snipers. What a blast-finger would have done to those
bloody carpets!"

The engineer showed signs of interest. "You're right!" he
snapped. "Blow 'em out of the sky—menace to life and limb!
I have a bill pending at the All Ellil Conference on Communication and Transportation—would you be interested?"

"No," grunted the general. The engineer, swishing his long
black cloak, returned to his throttle muttering about injunc-
tions and fair-play.

V

"Easy, now!" whispered the general.

"Yessir," answered a troll going through obvious mental strain while his hand, seemingly of its own volition, scrawled lines and symbols on a sheet of paper. Peter was watching, fascinated and mystified, as the specialist in military divination was doing his stuff.

"There!" said the troll, relaxing. He looked at the paper curiously and signed it: "Borgenssen, Capt."

"Well?" asked General Skaldberg. "What was it like?"

The Captain groaned. "You should see for yourself, sir!" he said despondently. "Their air-force is flying dragons and their infantry's a kind of Kraken squad. What they're doing out of water I don't know."

"Okay," said the general. He studied the drawing. "How about their mobility?"

"They haven't got any and they don't need any," complained the diviner. "They just sit there waiting for you—in a solid ring. And the air-force has a couple of auxiliary rocs that pick up the Krakens and drop them behind your forces. Pincher stuff—very bad."

"I'll be the judge of that!" said the general. The captain saluted and stumbled out of the little cave which the general had chosen to designate as GHQ. His men were bivouacked on the bare rock outside. Volcanoes rumbled and spat in the distance. There came one rolling crash that set Peter's hair on end.

"Think that was for us?" he asked nervously.

"Nope—I picked this spot for lava drainage. I have a hundred men erecting a shut-off at the only exposed point. We'll be safe enough." He turned again to the map, frowning. "This is our real worry—what I call impregnable, or damn near it. If we could get them to attack us—but those rocs smash anything along that line. We'd be cut off like a rosebud. And with our short munitions we can't afford to be discovered and surrounded. Ugh! What a spot for an army man to find himself in!"

A brassy female voice asked, "Somep'n bodderin' you, shorty?" The general spun around in a fine purple rage. Peter

looked in horror and astonishment on the immodest form of
a woman who had entered the cave entirely unperceived—
presumably by some occult means. She was a slutty creature, her hair dyed a vivid red and her satin skirt an inch or
two above the knee. She was violently made up with flame-
colored rouge, lipstick and even eye-shadow.

"Well," she complained stridently, puffing on a red cigaret,
"wadda you joiks gawkin' at? Aincha nevva seen a lady
befaw?"

"Madam," began the general, outraged.

"Can dat," she advised him easily. "I hoid youse guys
chewin' da fat. I wanna help youse out." She seated herself
on an outcropping of rock and adjusted her skirt upward.

"I concede that women," spluttered the general, "have their
place in activities of the military—but that place has little
or nothing to do with warfare as such! I demand that you
make yourself known—where did you come from?"

"Weh did I come from?" she asked mockingly. "Weh, he
wansa know. Lookit dat!" She pointed one of her bright-
glazed fingernails at the rocky floor of the cave, which grew
liquid in a moment, glowing cherry-red. She leered at the two
and spat at the floor. It grew cold in another moment. "Don't
dat mean nothin' to youse?" she asked.

The general stared at the floor. "You must be a volcano
nymph."

"Good fa you, shorty!" she sneered. "I represent da goils
from Local toity-tree. In brief, chums, our demands are dese:
one, dat youse clear away from our union hall pronto; two,
dat youse hang around in easy reach—in case we want youse
fa poiposes of our own. In return fa dese demands we—dats
me an' de goils—will help youse guys out against Almarish.
Dat lousy fink don't give his hands time off no more. Dis
place might as well be a desert fa all de men around. Get me?"

"These—ah—purposes of your own in clause two," said
the general hesitantly. "What would they be?"

She smiled and half-closed her eyes. "Escort soivice, ya
might call it, cap."

The general stared, too horrified even to resent being called
"cap."

"Well?" demanded the nymph.

"Well—yes," said the general.

"Okay, shorty," she said, crushing out her cigaret against

her palm. "Da goils'l be aroun' at dawn fa de attack. I'll try to keep 'em off yer army until de battle's over. So long!" She sank into the earth, leaving behind only a smell of fleur-de-floozy perfume.

"God!" whispered General Skaldberg. "The things I do for the army!"

In irregular open formation the trolls advanced, followed closely by the jeering mob of volcano nymphs.

"How about it, General?" asked Peter. He and the old soldier were surveying the field of battle from a hill in advance of their forces; the hideous octopoid forms of the defenders of Almarish could be plainly seen, lumbering onward to meet the trolls with a peculiar sucking gait.

"Any minute now—any second," said Skaldberg. Then, "Here it comes!" The farthest advanced of the trolls had met with the first of the Krakens. The creature lashed out viciously; Peter saw that its tentacles had been fitted with studded bands and other murderous devices. The troll dodged nimbly and pulled an invincible sword on the octopoid myth. They mixed it; when the struggle went behind an outcropping of rock the troll was in the lead, unharmed, while the slow-moving Kraken was leaking thinly from a score of punctures.

"The dragons," said Peter, pointing. "Here they are." In V formation the monsters were landing on a far end of the battlefield, then coming at a scrabbling run.

"If they make it quicker than the nymphs—" breathed the general. Then he sighed relievedly. They had not. The carnage among the dragons was almost funny; at will the nymphs lifted them high in the air on jets of steam and squirted melted rock in their eyes. Squalling in terror the dragons flapped into the air and lumbered off Southward.

"That's ocean," grinned the general. "They'll never come back—trying to find new homes, I suspect."

In an incredibly short time the field was littered with the flopping chunks that had been hewed from the Krakens. Living still they were, but powerless. The general shook his hand warmly. "You're on your own now," he said. "Good luck, boy. For a civilian you're not a bad egg at all." He walked away.

Glumly Peter surveyed the colossal fortress of Almarish. He walked aimlessly up to its gate, a huge thing of bronze and

silver, and pulled at the silken cord hanging there. A gong
sounded and the door swung open. Peter advanced hopelessly
in a sort of audience chamber. "So!" thundered a mighty
voice.

"So what?" asked Peter despondently. He saw on a throne
high above him an imposing figure. "You Almarish?" he asked
listlessly.

"I am. And who are you?"

"It doesn't matter. I'm Peter Packer of Braintree, Mass. I
don't even expect you to believe me. The throne lowered slowly
and jerkily, as if on hydraulic pumps. The wizard descended
and approached Peter. He was a man of about forty, with a
full brown beard reaching almost to his belt.

"Why," asked the sorcerer, "have you come bearing arms?"

"It's the only way I could come," said Peter. "Let me first
congratulate you on an efficient, well-oiled set of political machinery. Not even back in the United States have I seen graft
carried to such a high degree. Secondly, your choice of assis-
tants is an eye-opener. Your Mr. Pike is the neatest hench-
man I've ever seen. Thirdly, produce the person of Miss Melicent or I'll have to use force."

"Is that so?" rumbled Almarish. "Young puppy! I'd like to
see you try it. Wrestle with me—two falls out of three. I dare
you!"

Peter took off his coat of blue serge. "I never passed up a
dare yet," he said. "How about a mat?"

"Think I'm a sissy?" the sorcerer jeered.

Peter was stripped for action. "Okay," he said. Slowly
Almarish advanced on him, grappling for a hold. Peter let
him take his fore-arm, then shifted his weight so as to hurl
the magician over his shoulder. A moment later Peter was
astonished to find himself on the floor underneath the wizard.
"Haw!" grunted Almarish, rising. "You still game?" He braced
himself. "Yep!" snapped Peter. He hurled himself in a flying
tackle that began ten feet away from the wizard and ended
in a bone-crushing grip about the knees. Peter swarmed up
his trunk and cruelly twisted an arm across his chest. The
magician yelped in sudden agony, and let himself fall against
the floor. Peter rose, grinning. "One all," he said cheerfully.

Almarish grappled for the third fall; Peter cagily backed
away. The wizard hurled himself in a bruising body-block
against Peter, battering him off his feet and falling on the

young man. Instinctively Peter bridged his body, arching it off the floor. Almarish, grunting fiercely, gripped his arm and turned it slowly, as though he were winding a clock. Peter snapped over, rolling on the wizard's own body as a fulcrum. He had his toe in his hand, and closed his fist with every ounce of muscle he had. The sorcerer screamed and fell over on his face. Peter jammed his knee in the wizard's inside socket and bore down terribly. He could feel the bones bend in his grip.

"Enough!" gasped the wizard. Peter let him loose.

"You made it," said Almarish. "Two out of three."

Peter studied his face curiously. Take off that beard and you had—

"You said it, Grandfather Packer," said Peter, grinning.

Almarish groaned. "It's a wise child that knows its own father—grandfather, in this case," he said. "How could you tell?"

"Everything just clicked," said Peter simply. "You disappearing—that clock—somebody applying American methods in Ellil—and then I shaved you mentally and there you were. Simple?"

"Sure is. But how do you think I made out here, boy?"

"Shamefully. That kind of thing isn't tolerated any more. It's gangsterism—you'll have to cut it out, gramp."

"Gangsterism be damned!" snorted the wizard. "It's business. Business and common-sense."

"Business maybe, certainly not common-sense. My boys wiped out your guard and I might have wiped out you if I had magic stronger than yours."

Grandfather Packer chuckled in glee. "Magic? I'll begin at the beginning. When I got that dad-blamed clock back in '63 I dropped right into Ellil—onto the head of an assassin who was going for a real magician. Getting the set-up I pinned the killer with a half-nelson and the magician dispatched him. Then he got grateful, said he was retiring from public life and gave me a kind of token, good for any three wishes.

"So I took it, thanking him kindly, and wished for a palace and bunch of gutty retainers. It was in my mind to run Ellil like a business, and I did it the only way I knew how—force. And from that day to this I used only one wish and I haven't a dab of magic more than that!"

"I'll be damned!" whispered Peter.

"And you know what I'm going to do with those other two wishes? I'm going to take you and me right back into the good ole U.S.A.!"

"Will it only send two people?"

"So the magician said."

"Grandfather Packer," said Peter earnestly, "I am about to ask a very great sacrifice of you. It is also your duty to undo the damage which you have done."

"Oh," said Almarish glumly. "The girl? All right."

"You don't mind?" asked Peter incredulously.

"Far be it from me to stand in the way of young love," grunted the wizard sourly. "She's up there."

Peter entered timidly; the girl was alternately reading a copy of the *Braintree Informer* and staring passionately at a photograph of Peter.

"Darling," said Peter.

"Dearest!" said Melicent, catching on almost immediately.

A short while later Peter was asking her: "Do you mind, dearest if I ask one favor of you—a very great sacrifice?" He produced a small, sharp pen-knife.

And all the gossip for a month in Braintree was of Peter Packer's stunning young wife, though some people wondered how it was that she had only nine fingers.

The Goodly Creatures

How many goodly creatures are there here!
How beauteous mankind is! O brave new world,
That has such people in 't!
                    Miranda in The Tempest

FARWELL suddenly realized that his fingers had been trembling all morning, with a hair-fine vibration that he couldn't control. He looked at them in amazement and rested them on the keys of his typewriter. The tremor stopped and Farwell told himself to ignore it; then it would go away. The copy in the typewriter said: *Kumfyseets—add 1* in the upper left-hand corner and under it:—*hailed by veteran spacemen as the greatest advance in personal comfort and safety on the spaceways since—*

Since what? It was just another pneumatic couch. Why didn't he ever get anything he could *work* with? This one begged for pix—a stripped-down model in a Kumfyseet, smiling under a pretended seven-G takeoff acceleration—but the Chicago Chair Company account didn't have an art budget. No art, and they were howling for tear-sheets already.

— *comfort and safety on the spaceways since—*

He could take Worple to a good lunch and get a shirt-tail graf in his lousy "Stubby Says" column and that should hold Chicago Chair for another week. They wouldn't know the difference between Worple and—

Farwell's intercom buzzed. "Mr. Henry Schneider to see you about employment."

"Send him in, Grace."

Schneider was a beefy kid with a practiced smile and a heavy handshake. "I saw your ad for a junior copywriter," he

75

said, sitting down confidently. He opened an expensive, new-looking briefcase and threw a folder on the desk.

Farwell leafed through it—the standard presentation. A fact sheet listing journalistic honors in high school and college, summer jobs on weeklies, "rose to sergeantcy in only ten months during U.M.T. period." Copies of by-line pieces pasted neatly, without wrinkles, onto heavy pages. A TV scenario for the college station. A letter from the dean of men, a letter from the dean of the journalism school.

"As you see," Schneider told him, "I'm versatile. Sports, travel, science, human-interest, spot news—anything."

"Yes. Well, you wouldn't be doing much actual writing to start, Schneider. When—"

"I'm glad you mentioned that, Mr. Farwell. What exactly would be the nature of my work?"

"The usual *cursus honorum*—" Schneider looked blank and then laughed heartily. Farwell tried again: "The usual success story in public relations is, copy boy to junior copywriter to general copywriter to accounts man to executive. If you last that long. For about three months you can serve Greenhough and Brady best by running copy, emptying waste baskets and keeping your eyes open. After you know the routine we can try you on—"

Schneider interrupted: "What's the policy on salaries?" He didn't seem to like the policy on promotions.

Farwell told him the policy on salaries and Schneider tightened his mouth disapprovingly. "That's not much for a starter," he said. "Of course, I don't want to haggle, but I think my presentation shows I can handle responsibility."

Farwell got up with relief and shook his hand. "Too bad we couldn't get together," he said, talking the youngster to the door. "Don't forget your briefcase. If you want, you can leave your name with the girl and we'll get in touch with you if anything comes up. As you say, you might do better in another outfit that has a more responsible job open. It was good of you to give us a try, Schneider . . ." A warm clap on the shoulder got him out.

Next time, Farwell thought, feeling his 45 years, it would be better to mention the starting salary in the ad and short-stop the youngsters with inflated ideas. He was pretty sure he hadn't acted like that beefy hotshot when he was a kid—or had he?

—*comfort and safety on the spaceways since*—

He turned on the intercom and said: "Get me Stubby Worple at the *Herald*."

Worple was in.

"Jim Farwell, Stub. I was looking at the column this morning and I made myself a promise to buzz you and tell you what a damn fine job it is. The lead graf was sensational."

Modest protests.

"No, I mean it. Say, why don't we get together? You got anything on for lunch?"

He did, but how about dinner? Hadn't been to the Mars Room for a coon's age.

"Oh, Mars Room. Sure enough all right with me. Meet you in the bar at 7:30?"

He would.

Well, he'd left himself wide open for that one. He'd be lucky to get off with a $30 tab. But it was a sure tear-sheet for the Chicago Chair people.

Farwell said to the intercom: "Get me a reservation for 8 tonight at the Mars Room, Grace. Dinner for two. Tell Mario it's got to be a good table."

He ripped the Kumfyseets first ad out of the typewriter and dropped it into the waste basket. Fifty a week from Chicago Chair less 30 for entertainment. Mr. Brady wasn't going to like it; Mr. Brady might call him from New York about it to say gently: "Anybody can *buy* space, Jim. You should know by now that we're not in the business of *buying* space. Sometimes I think you haven't got a grasp of the big picture the way a branch manager should. Greenhough asked about you the other day and I really didn't know what to tell him." And Farwell would sweat and try to explain how it was a special situation and maybe try to hint that the sales force was sometimes guilty of overselling a client, making promises that Ops couldn't possibly live up to. And Mr. Brady would close on a note of gentle melancholy with a stinging remark or two "for your own good, Jim."

Farwell glanced at the clock on his desk, poured one from his private bottle; Brady receded a little into the background of his mind.

"Mr. Angelo Libonari to see you," said the intercom. "About employment."

"Send him in."

Libonari stumbled on the carpeting that began at the threshold of Farwell's office. "I saw your ad," he began shrilly, "your ad for a junior copywriter."

"Have a seat." The boy was shabby and jittery. "Didn't you bring a presentation?"

He didn't understand. "No, I just saw your ad. I didn't know I had to be introduced. I'm sorry I took up your time—" He was on his way out already.

"*Wait* a minute, Angelo! I meant, have you got any copies of what you've done, where you've been to school, things like that."

"Oh." The boy pulled out a sheaf of paper from his jacket pocket. "This stuff isn't very good," he said. "As a matter of fact, it isn't really finished. I wrote it for a magazine, *Integration*, I don't suppose you ever heard of it; they were going to print it but they folded up, it's a kind of prose poem." Abruptly he ran dry and handed over the wad of dog-eared, interlined copy. His eyes said to Farwell: *please don't laugh at me.*

Farwell read at random: "—and then the Moon will drift astern and out of sight, the broken boundary that used to stand between the eye and the mind." He read it aloud and asked: "Now, what does that mean?"

The boy shyly and proudly explained: "Well, what I was trying to bring out there was that the Moon used to be as far as anybody could go with his eyes. If you wanted to find out anything about the other celestial bodies you had to guess and make inductions—that's sort of the whole theme of the piece—liberation, broken boundaries."

"Uh-huh," said Farwell, and went on reading. It was a rambling account of an Earth-Ganymede flight. There was a lot of stuff as fuzzy as the first bit, there were other bits that were hard, clean writing. The kid might be worth developing if only he didn't look and act so *peculiar*. Maybe it was just nervousness.

"So you're specially interested in space travel?" he asked.

"Oh, very much. I know I failed to get it over in this; it's all second-hand. I've never been off. But nobody's really written well about it yet—" He froze.

His terrible secret, Farwell supposed with amusement, was that he hoped to be the laureate of space flight. Well, if he wasn't absolutely impossible, Greenhough and Brady could

give him a try. Shabby as he was, he wouldn't dare quibble
about the pay.

He didn't quibble. He told Farwell he could get along on it
nicely, he had a room in the run-down sub-Bohemian near
north side of town. He was from San Francisco, but had left
home years ago—Farwell got the idea that he'd run away—
and been in a lot of places. He'd held a lot of menial jobs
and picked up a few credits taking night college courses here
and there. After a while Farwell told him he was hired and to
see the girl for his withholding tax and personnel data forms.

He buzzed his copy chief about the boy and leaned back
in good humor. Angelo could never get to be an accounts man,
of course, but he had some talent and imagination. Tame it
and the kid could grow into a good producer. A rocket fan
would be handy to have around if Sales stuck Ops with any
more lemons like Chicago Chair.

Worple drank that night at the Mars Room like a man with
a hollow leg and Farwell more or less had to go along with
him. He got the Kumfyseets item planted but arrived at the
office late and queasy as McGuffy, the copy chief, was bawling
out Angelo for showing up in a plaid shirt, and a dirty one
at that.

McGuffy came in to see him at 4:30 to ask about Angelo.
"He just doesn't seem to be a Greenhough and Brady man,
J. F. Of course if you think he's got something on the ball,
that's good enough for me. But, honestly, can you see him taking an account to lunch?"

"Is he really getting in your hair, Mac? Give him a few
days."

McGuffy was back at the end of the week, raging. "He
showed me a poem, J. F. A sonnet about Mars. And he acted
as if he was doing me a favor! As if he was handing me a contract with Panamerican Steel!"

Farwell laughed; it was exactly what he would expect Angelo to do. "It was his idea of a compliment, Mac. It means
he thinks you're a good critic. I know these kids. I used to—"
He broke off, dead-pan.

McGuffy grumbled: "You know I'm loyal, J. F. If you think
he's got promise, all right. But he's driving me nuts."

After the copy chief left, Farwell shook his head nervously.
What had he almost said? "I used to be one myself." Why,

so he had—just about 25 years ago, a quarter of a century ago, when he went into radio work temporarily. *Temporarily!* A quarter-century ago he had been twenty years old. A quarter-century ago he had almost flunked out of college because he sat up all night trying to write plays instead of studying.

He hazily remembered saying to somebody, a girl, something like: "I am aiming for a really creative synthesis of Pinero and Shaw." Somehow that stuck, but he couldn't remember what the girl looked like or whether she'd been impressed. Farwell felt his ears burning: "A really creative synthesis of Pinero and Shaw." What a little————!

He told the intercom: "Send in Libonari."

The boy was more presentable; his hair was cut and he wore a clean blue shirt. "I've had a couple of complaints," said Farwell. "Suppose we get this clear: you are the one who is going to conform if you want to stay with us. Greenhough and Brady isn't going to be remolded nearer to the heart's desire of Angelo Libonari. Are you going out of your way to be difficult?"

The boy shrugged uneasily and stammered: "No, I wouldn't do anything like that. It's just, it's just that I find it hard to take all this seriously—but don't misunderstand me. I mean I can't help thinking that I'm going to do more important things some day, but honestly, I'm trying to do a good job here."

"Well, honestly you'd better try harder," Farwell said, mimicking his nervous voice. And then, more agreeably: "I'm not saying this for fun, Angelo. I just don't want to see you wasted because you won't put out a little effort, use a little self-discipline. You've got a future here if you work with us instead of against us. If you keep rubbing people the wrong way and I have to fire you, what's it going to be? More hash-house jobs, more crummy furnished rooms, hot in the summer, cold in the winter. You'll have something you call 'freedom,' but it's not the real thing. And it's all you'll have. Now beat it and try not to get on Mr. McGuffy's nerves."

The boy left, looking remorseful, and Farwell told himself that not everybody could handle an out-of-the-way type that well. If he pasted the little sermon in his hat he'd be all right.

"Really creative synthesis!" Farwell snorted and poured himself a drink before he buckled down to planning a series of releases for the International Spacemen's Union. The space lines, longing for the old open-shop days, were sniping at the

I.S.U. wherever they found an opening. They had a good one in the unions' high initiation fee. The union said the high fee kept waifs and strays out and insured that anybody who paid it meant business and would make the spaceways his career. The union said the benefits that flowed from this were many and obvious. The companies said the union just wanted the money.

Farwell started blocking out a midwestern campaign. It might start with letters to the papers signed by SPACEMAN'S WIFE, WIDOW OF SCAB SPACER and other folks; the union could locate them to sign the letters. Next thing to do was set up a disinterested outfit. He tentatively christened it "The First Pan-American Conference on Space Hazards" and jotted down the names of a few distinguished chronic joiners and sponsors for the letterheads. They could hold a three-day meeting in Chicago, and conclude that the most important factor in space safety is experienced crewmen, and the longer their service the better. No mention of the I.S.U. initiation fee policy out of the F.P.A.C.S.H., but the union could use their conclusions in *its* material.

The union could use it to get a couple of state legislatures to pass resolutions endorsing the initiation fee policy. G. & B. would write the resolutions, but the I.S.U.—an independent union—would have to swing the big federations into putting pressure on the legislatures in the name of labor unity.

Numerically the spacemen were insignificant.

He pawed through stacks of material forwarded to him as ammo by the union looking for the exact amount of fee but couldn't locate it. The coyness was not surprising; it recalled the way corporation handouts bannered the "profit per dollar of sales" and buried the total profit in dollars and cents. He buzzed Copy.

"Mac, does anybody there know exactly what the I.S.U. initiation fee is?"

"I'll see, J. F."

A moment later he heard Angelo's voice. "It's kind of complicated, Mr. Farwell—maybe to keep anybody from saying it's exactly this or exactly that. Here's the way it works: base fee, $1000, to be paid before they issue you a work card. What they call 'accrual fee' on top of that—$100 if you're twenty years old, $200 if you're twenty-two, $300 if you're twenty-four and so on up to 30, and after that you can't

join. You can pay accrual fee out of your first voyage. *From
the accrual fee you can deduct $50 for each dependent.* On
top of that there's a 5 per cent assessment of your first-voyage
pay only, earmarked for the I.S.U. Space Medicine Research
Foundation at Johns Hopkins. And that's all."

Farwell had been jotting it down. "Thanks, Angelo," he said
absently. The Space Medicine Research thing was good, but
he'd have to be careful that they weren't represented at the
F.P.A.C.S.H.; you didn't want a direct union tie-in there. Now
what could you do about the fee? Get the union to dig up
somebody who's paid only the $1000 base because of age and
the right number of dependents. Forget the accrual and the
assessment. How many people on a space ship—50, 60? Make
it 60 to get a plausibly unround number. Sixty into 1000 is
$16^{67}/_{100}$.

"Dear Editor: Is there anybody riding the spaceways who
would not cheerfully pay $16.67 cents to insure that the
crewmen who hold his life in their hands are thoroughly experienced veterans of interplanetary flight? Is there anybody
so short-sighted that he would embark with a green crew to
save $16.67? Of course not! And yet that is what certain
short-sighted persons demand! Throwing up a smoke-screen of
loose charges to divert the public from the paramount issue
of *SAFETY* they accuse—"

That wasn't exactly it. He had made it look as though the
passengers paid the I.S.U. initiation fee. Well, he'd struck a
keynote; Copy could take it from there.

And then there ought to be a stunt—a good, big stunt with
pix possibilities. Girls, or violence, or both. Maybe a model
demonstrating an escape hatch or something at a trade show,
something goes wrong, a heroic I.S.U. member in good standing who happens to be nearby dashes in—

He was feeling quite himself again.

The switchboard girl must have been listening in on the New
York call. As Farwell stepped from his office he felt electricity
in the air; the word had been passed already. He studied the
anteroom, trying to see it through Greenhough's eyes.

"Grace," he told the switchboard girl, "get your handbag
off the PBX and stick it in a drawer somewhere. Straighten
that picture. And put on your bolero—you have nice shoulders
and we all appreciate them, but the office is air-conditioned."

She tried to look surprised as he went on into Art.

Holoway didn't bother to pretend. "What time's he getting in?" he asked worriedly. "Can I get a shave?"

"They didn't tell me," said Farwell. "Your shave's all right. Get things picked up and get ties on the boys." The warning light was off; he looked into the darkroom. "A filthy mess!" he snapped. "How can you get any work done in a litter like that? Clean it up."

"Right away, J. F.," Holoway said, hurt.

Copy was in better shape; McGuffy had a taut hand.

"Greenhough's coming in today, I don't know what time. Your boys here look good."

"I can housebreak anything, J. F. Even Angelo. He bought a new suit!"

Farwell allowed a slight puzzled look to cross his face. "Angelo? Oh, the Libonari boy. How's he doing?"

"No complaints. He'll never be an accounts man if I'm any judge, but I've been giving him letters to write the past couple weeks. I don't know how you spotted it, but he's got talent. I have to hand it to you for digging him up, J. F."

Farwell saw the boy now at the last desk on the windowless side of the room, writing earnestly in longhand. Two months on a fair-enough salary hadn't filled him out as much as Farwell expected, but he did have a new suit on his back.

"It was just a gamble," he told McGuffy and went back to his office.

He had pretended not to remember the kid. Actually he'd been in his thoughts off and on since he hired him. There had been no trouble with Angelo since his grim little interview with the boy. Farwell hoped, rather sentimentally, he knew, that the interview had launched him on a decent career, turned him aside from the rocky Bohemian road and its pitfalls. As he had been turned aside himself. The nonsensical "really creative synthesis of Pinero and Shaw" pattered through his head again and he winced, thoroughly sick of it. For the past week the thought of visiting a psychiatrist had pattered after Pinero and Shaw every time, each time to be dismissed as silly.

His phone buzzed and he mechanically said, "Jim Farwell."

"Farwell, why didn't you check with me?" rasped Greenhough's voice.

"I don't understand, Mr. Greenhough. Where are you calling from?"

"The Hotel Greybar down the street, of course! I've been sitting here for an hour waiting for your call."

"Mr. Greenhough, all they told me from New York was that you were coming to Chicago."

"Nonsense. I gave the instructions myself."

"I'm sorry about the mixup—I must have misunderstood. Are you going to have a look at the office?"

"No. Why should I do anything like that? I'll call you back." Greenhough hung up.

Farwell leaned back, cursing whoever in New York had crossed up the message. It had probably been done deliberately, he decided—Pete Messler, the New York office manager trying to make him look bad.

He tried to work on an account or two, but nervously put them aside to wait for Greenhough's call. At 5 he tried to reach Greenhough to tell him he was going home and give him his home number. Greenhough's room didn't answer the call or his next four, so he phoned a drugstore to send up a sandwich and coffee.

Before he could get started on the sandwich Greenhough phoned again to invite him to dinner at the Mars Room. He was jovial as could be: "Get myself some of that famous Chicago hospitality, hey, Jim? You know I'm just a hick from Colorado, don't you?" He went on to give Farwell about ten minutes of chuckling reminiscence and then hung up without confirming the dinner date. It turned out that it didn't matter. As Farwell was leaving the deserted office his phone buzzed again. It was Greenhough abruptly calling off the Mars Room. He told Farwell: "I've got somebody important to talk to this evening."

The branch manager at last dared to pour himself a heavy drink and left.

His bedside phone shrilled at 3 in the morning. "Jim Farwell," he croaked into it while two clock dials with the hands making two luminous L's wavered in front of him. His drink at the office had been the first of a series.

"This is Greenhough, Farwell," snarled the voice of the senior partner. "You get over here right away. Bring Clancy, whatever his name is—the lawyer." *Click.*

Where was "here"? Farwell phoned the Greybar. *"Don't connect me with his room—I just want to know if he's in."*

The floor clerk said he was and Farwell tried to phone the home of the Chicago branch's lawyer, but got no answer. Too much time lost. He soaked his head in cold water, threw his clothes on and drove hell-for-leather to the Greybar.

Greenhough was in one of the big two-bedroom suites on the sixteenth floor. A frozen-faced blond girl in an evening gown let Farwell in without a word. The senior partner was sprawled on the sofa in dress trousers and stiff shirt. He had a bruise under his left eye.

"I came as quickly as I could, Mr. Greenhough," said Farwell. "I couldn't get in touch with—"

The senior partner coughed thunderously, twitched his face at Farwell in a baffling manner, and then stalked into a bedroom. The blond girl's frozen mask suddenly split into a vindictive grin. "*You're* going to get it!" she jeered at Farwell. "I'm supposed to think his name's Wilkins. Well, go on after him, pappy."

Farwell went into the bedroom. Greenhough was sitting on the bed dabbing at the bruise and muttering. "I told you I wanted our lawyer!" he shouted at the branch manager. "I was attacked by a drunkard in that damned Mars Room of yours and by God booked by the police like a common criminal! I'm going to get satisfaction if I have to turn the city upsidedown! Get on that phone and get me Clancy or whatever his name is!"

"But I *can't!*" said Farwell desperately. "He won't answer his phone and in the second place he isn't that kind of lawyer. I *can't* ask Clarahan to fight a disorderly-conduct charge— he's a big man here. He only does contract law and that kind of thing. You posted bond, didn't you, Mr. Greenhough?"

"Twenty dollars," said the senior partner bitterly, "and they only wanted ten from that drunken ape."

"Then why not just forget about it? Forfeit the bond and probably you'll never hear of it again, especially since you're an out-of-towner. I'll do what I can to smooth it over if they don't let it slide."

"Get out of here," said Greenhough, dabbing at the bruise again.

The blond was reading a TV magazine in the parlor; she ignored Farwell as he let himself out.

The branch manager drove to an all-night barber shop near

one of the terminals and napped through "the works." A slow breakfast killed another hour and by then it wasn't too ridiculously early to appear at the office.

He dawdled over copy until 9 and phoned the Greybar. They told him Mr. Greenhough had checked out leaving no forwarding address. The morning papers came and he found nothing about a scuffle at the Mars Room or the booking of Greenhough. Maybe the senior partner had given a false name—Wilkins?—or maybe the stories had been killed because Greenhough and Brady did some institutional advertising. Maybe there was some mysterious interlock between Greenhough and Brady and the papers high up on some misty alp that Farwell had never glimpsed.

Don't worry about it, he told himself savagely. You gave him good advice, the thing's going to blow over, Clarahan wouldn't have taken it anyway. He hoped Pete Messler in New York wouldn't hear about it and try to use it as a lever to pry him out of the spot he held, the spot Pete Messler coveted. Maybe there was some way he could get somebody in the New York office to keep an eye on Messler and let him know how he was doing, just to get something he could counterpunch with when Messler pulled something like that garbled message stunt.

The intercom buzzed and Grace said, "Angelo wants to see you. He says it's personal."

"Send him in."

The kid was beaming. He looked pretty good—not raw and jumpy; just happy.

"I want to say thanks and good-bye, Mr. Farwell," he told the branch manager. "Look!"

The plastic-laminated card said "WORK PERMIT" and "Brother Angelo Libonari" and "International Union of Spacemen, Spacedockworkers and Rocket Maintenance Men, Unaffiliated (ISU-IND)" and "Member in Good Standing" and other things.

"So that was the game," said Farwell slowly. "We take you and we train you at a loss hoping that some day you'll turn out decent copy for us and as soon as you have a thousand bucks saved up you quit like a shot and buy a work card to be a wiper on a rocket. Well, I hope you show a little more loyalty to your space line than you showed us."

Angelo's face drooped in miserable surprise. "I never thought—" he stuttered. "I didn't mean to run out, Mr. Farwell. I'll give two weeks notice if you want—a month? How about a month?"

"It doesn't matter," said Farwell. "I should have known. I thought I pounded some sense into your head, but I was wrong. You're forgiven, Angelo. I hope you have a good time. What are your plans?" He wasn't really interested, but why go out of his way to kick the kid in the teeth? Obviously he'd meant it when he registered surprise—he didn't have the boss's viewpoint and his other jobs had been one-week stands in hashhouses.

The boy carefully put his work card in his breast pocket and beamed again at what he was saying—partly to Farwell, it appeared, mostly to himself in wonder at its coming true at last. "I'll be a wiper at the start, all right," he said. "I don't care if I never get higher than that. I want to see it and feel it, all of it. That's the only way the real thing's ever going to get written. Higgins and Delare and Beeman and the rest of them—passengers. You can feel it in your bones when you read their stuff. One-trippers or two-trippers.

"They aren't soaked in it. The big passage in Delare's *Planetfall*, the takeoff from Mars: he's full of the wonder of it, sure. Who wouldn't be the first time? And he kept his eyes open, watching himself and the others. But I'm going to take off from Earth and Mars and Venus and Ganymede and the Moon twenty times before I dare to write about it. I'm going to get it *all*—brains, bone, muscle, and belly—takeoff, landings, free flight, danger, monotony—*all* of it."

"Sonnets? Prose poems?" asked Farwell, just to be saying something.

Angelo flushed a little, but his eyes didn't have the old pleading look. He didn't have to plead; he had what he wanted. "They were good exercise," he said stoutly. "I suppose I was trying to write form because I didn't have content. I think it's going to be novels—if I feel like it. And they can publish them or not publish them, just as they please." He meant it, Farwell thought. He had what he wanted.

"I'll look forward to them," he said, and shook hands with the boy. He didn't notice him leave. Angelo Messler, he thought; Pete Libonari. "—really creative synthesis of Pinero and Shaw—" pattered through his head, and the psychiatrist-thought followed naggingly after. He looked at his hands in amazement, suddenly realizing that they had been trembling all morning uncontrollably.

Friend to Man

CALL him, if anything, Smith. He had answered to that and to other names in the past. Occupation, fugitive. His flight, it is true, had days before slowed to a walk and then to a crawl, but still he moved, a speck of gray, across the vast and featureless red plain of a planet not his own.

Nobody was following Smith, he sometimes realized, and then he would rest for a while, but not long. After a minute or an hour the posse of his mind would reform and spur behind him; reason would cry no and still he would heave himself to his feet and begin again to inch across the sand.

The posse, imaginary and terrible, faded from front to rear. Perhaps in the very last rank of pursuers was a dim shadow of a schoolmate. Smith had never been one to fight fair. More solid were the images of his first commercial venture, the hijacking job. A truck driver with his chest burned out namelessly pursued; by his side a faceless cop. The ranks of the posse grew crowded then, for Smith had been a sort of organizer after that, but never an organizer too proud to demonstrate his skill. An immemorially old-fashioned garrotting-wire trailed inches from the nape of Winkle's neck, for Winkle had nearly sung to the police.

"Squealer!" shrieked Smith abruptly, startling himself. Shaking, he closed his eyes and still Winkle plodded after him, the tails of wire bobbing with every step, stiffly.

A solid, businesslike patrolman eclipsed him, drilled through the throat; beside him was the miraculously resurrected shade of Henderson.

The twelve-man crew of a pirated lighter marched, as you would expect, in military formation, but they bled ceaselessly

89

from their ears and eyes as people do when shot into space without helmets.

These he could bear, but, somehow, Smith did not like to look at the leader of the posse. It was odd, but he did not like to look at her.

She had no business there! If they were ghosts why was she there? He hadn't killed her, and, as far as he knew, Amy was alive and doing business in the Open Quarter at Portsmouth. It wasn't fair, Smith wearily thought. He inched across the featureless plain and Amy followed with her eyes.

> *Let us! Let us! We have waited so long!*
> *Wait longer, little ones. Wait longer.*

Smith, arriving at the planet, had gravitated to the Open Quarter and found, of course, that his reputation had preceded him. Little, sharp-faced men had sidled up to pay their respects, and they happened to know of a job waiting for the right touch—

He brushed them off.

Smith found the virginal, gray-eyed Amy punching tapes for the Transport Company, tepidly engaged to a junior executive. The daughter of the Board Chairman, she fancied herself daring to work in the rough office at the port.

First was the child's play of banishing her young man. A minor operation, it was managed with the smoothness and dispatch one learns after years of such things. Young Square-Jaw had been quite willing to be seduced by a talented young woman from the Open Quarter, and had been so comically astonished when the photographs appeared on the office bulletin board!

He had left by the next freighter, sweltering in a bunk by the tube butts, and the forlorn gray eyes were wet for him.

> *But how much longer must we wait?*
> *Much longer, little ones. It is weak—too weak.*

The posse, Smith thought vaguely, was closing in. That meant, he supposed, that he was dying. It would not be too bad to be dead, quickly and cleanly. He had a horror of filth.

Really, he thought, this was too bad! The posse was in front of him—

It was not the posse; it was a spindly, complicated creature that, after a minute of bleary staring, he recognized as a native of the planet.

Smith thought and thought as he stared and could think of nothing to do about it. The problem was one of the few that he had never considered and debated within himself. If it had been a cop he would have acted; if it had been any human being he would have acted, but this—

He could think of nothing more logical to do than to lie down, pull the hood across his face and go to sleep.

He woke in an underground chamber big enough for half a dozen men. It was egg-shaped and cool, illuminated by sunlight red-filtered through the top half. He touched the red-lit surface and found it to be composed of glass marbles cemented together with a translucent plastic. The marbles he knew; the red desert was full of them, wind-polished against each other for millennia, rarely perfectly round, as all of these were. They had been most carefully collected. The bottom half of the egg-shaped cave was a mosaic of flatter, opaque pebbles, cemented with the same plastic.

Smith found himself thinking clear, dry, level thoughts. The posse was gone and he was sane and there had been a native and this must be the native's burrow. He had been cached there as food, of course, so he would kill the native and possibly drink its body fluids, for his canteen had been empty for a long time. He drew a knife and wondered how to kill, his eyes on the dark circle which led from the burrow to the surface.

Silently the dark circle was filled with the tangled appendages of the creature, and in the midst of the appendages was, insanely, a Standard Transport Corporation five liter can.

The STC monogram had been worn down, but was unmistakable. The can had heft to it.

Water? The creature seemed to hold it out. He reached into the tangle and the can was smoothly released to him. The catch flipped up and he drank flat, distilled water in great gulps.

He felt that he bulged with the stuff when he stopped, and knew the first uneasy intimations of inevitable cramp. The native was not moving, but something that could have been an eye turned on him.

"Salt?" asked Smith, his voice thin in the thin air. "I need salt with water."

The thing rubbed two appendages together and he saw a drop of amber exude and spread on them. It was, he realized a moment later, rosining the bow, for the appendages drew across each other and he heard a whining, vibrating cricket-voice say: "S-s-z-z-aw-w?"

"Salt," said Smith.

It did better the next time. The amber drop spread, and— "S-z-aw-t?" was sounded, with a little tap of the bow for the final phoneme.

It vanished, and Smith leaned back with the cramps beginning. His stomach convulsed and he lost the water he had drunk. It seeped without a trace into the floor. He doubled up and groaned—once. The groan had not eased him in body or mind; he would groan no more but let the cramps run their course.

Nothing but what is useful had always been his tacit motto. There had not been a false step in the episode of Amy. When Square-Jaw had been disposed of, Smith had waited until her father, perhaps worldly enough to know his game, certain at all events not to like the way he played it, left on one of his regular inspection trips. He had been formally introduced to her by a mutual friend who owed money to a dangerous man in the Quarter, but who had not yet been found out by the tight little clique that thought it ruled the commercial world of that planet.

With precision he had initiated her into the Open Quarter by such easy stages that at no one point could she ever suddenly realize that she was in it or the gray eyes ever fill with shock. Smith had, unknown to her, disposed of some of her friends, chosen other new ones, stage-managed entire days for her, gently forcing opinions and attitudes, insistent, withdrawing at the slightest token of counter-pressure, always urging again when the counter-pressure relaxed.

The night she had taken Optol had been prepared for by a magazine article—notorious in the profession as a whitewash—a chance conversation in which chance did not figure at all, a televised lecture on addiction, and a trip to an Optol joint at which everybody had been gay and healthy. On the second visit, Amy had pleaded for the stuff—just out of curiosity, of course, and he had reluctantly called the unfrocked medic, who injected the gray eyes with the oil.

It had been worth his minute pains; he had got 200 feet of

film while she staggered and reeled loathesomely. And she had, after the Optol evaporated, described with amazed delight how *different* everything had looked, and how exquisitely she had danced. . . .

"S-z-aw-t!" announced the native from the mouth of the burrow. It bowled at him marbles of rock-salt from the surface, where rain never fell to dissolve them.

He licked one, then cautiously sipped water. He looked at the native, thought, and put his knife away. It came into the burrow and reclined at the opposite end from Smith.

It knows what a knife is, and water and salt, and something about language, he thought between sips. What's the racket?

> But when? But when?
> Wait longer, little ones. Wait longer.

"You understand me?" Smith asked abruptly.

The amber drop exuded, and the native played whiningly: "*A-ah-nn-nah-t-ann*."

"Well," said Smith, "thanks."

He never really knew where the water came from, but guessed that it had been distilled in some fashion within the body of the native. He had, certainly, seen the thing shovel indiscriminate loads of crystals into its mouth—calcium carbonate, aluminum hydroxide, anything—and later emit amorphous powders from one vent and water from another. His food, brought on half an STC can, was utterly unrecognizable —a jelly, with bits of crystal embedded in it that he had to spit out.

What it did for a living was never clear. It would lie for hours in torpor, disappear on mysterious errands, bring him food and water, sweep out the burrow with a specialized limb, converse when requested.

It was days before Smith really *saw* the creature. In the middle of a talk with it he recognized it as a fellow organism rather than as a machine, or gadget, or nightmare, or alien monster. It was, for Smith, a vast step to take.

Not easily he compared his own body with the native's, and admitted that, of course, his was inferior. The cunning jointing of the limbs, the marvelously practical detail of the eye, the economy of the external muscle system, were admirable.

Now and then at night the posse would return and crowd about him as he lay dreaming, and he knew that he screamed then, reverberatingly in the burrow. He awoke to find the most humanoid of the native's limbs resting on his brow, soothingly, and he was grateful for the new favor; he had begun to take his food and water for granted.

The conversations with the creature were whimsy as much as anything else. It was, he thought, the rarest of Samaritans, who had no interest in the private life of its wounded wayfarer.

He told it of life in the cities of the planet, and it sawed out politely that the cities were very big indeed. He told it of the pleasures of human beings, and it politely agreed that their pleasures were most pleasant.

Under its cool benevolence he stammered and faltered in his ruthlessness. On the nights when he woke screaming and was comforted by it he would demand to know why it cared to comfort him.

It would saw out: "*S-z-lee-p mm-ah-ee-nn-d s-z-rahng.*" And from that he could conjecture that sound sleep makes the mind strong, or that the mind must be strong for the body to be strong, or whatever else he wished. It was *kindness,* he knew, and he felt shifty and rotted when he thought of, say, Amy.

> *It will be soon, will it not? Soon?*
> *Quite soon, little ones. Quite, quite soon.*

Amy had not fallen; she had been led, slowly, carefully, by the hand. She had gone delightfully down, night after night. He had been amused to note that there was a night not long after the night of Optol when he had urged her to abstain from further indulgence in a certain diversion which had no name that anyone used, an Avernian pleasure the penalties against which were so severe that one would not compromise himself so far as admitting that he knew it existed and was practiced. Smith had urged her to abstain, and had most sincerely this time meant it. She was heading for the inevitable collapse, and her father was due back from his inspection tour. The whole process had taken some fifty days.

Her father, another gray-eyed booby. . . . A projection

room. "A hoax." "Fifty thousand in small, unmarked. . . ." The flickering reel-change. "It *can't* be—" "You should know that scar." "I'll kill you first!" "That won't burn the prints." The lights. "The last one—I don't believe. . . ." "Fifty thousand." "I'll kill you—"

But he hadn't. He'd killed himself, for no good reason that Smith could understand. Disgustedly, no longer a blackmailer, much out of pocket by this deal that had fizzled, he turned hawker and peddled prints of the film to the sort of person who would buy such things. He almost got his expenses back. After the week of concentration on his sudden mercantile enterprise, he had thought to inquire about Amy.

She had had her smashup, lost her job tape-punching now that her father was dead and her really scandalous behavior could no longer be ignored. She had got an unconventional job in the Open Quarter. She had left it. She appeared, hanging around the shops at Standard Transport, where the watchmen had orders to drive her away. She always came back, and one day, evidently, got what she wanted.

For on the Portsmouth-Jamestown run, which Smith was making to see a man who had a bar with a small theater in what was ostensibly a storeroom, his ship had parted at the seams.

"Dumped me where you found me—mid-desert."

"T-urr-ss-t-ee," sawed the native.

There seemed to be some reproach in the word, and Smith chided himself for imagining that a creature which spoke by stridulation could charge its language with the same emotional overtones as those who used lungs and vocal cords.

But there the note was again: "Ei-m-m-ee—t-urr-ss-t—t-oo."

Amy thirst too. A stridulating moralist. But still . . . one had to admit . . . in his frosty way, Smith was reasoning, but a wash of emotion blurred the diagrams, the cold diagrams by which he had always lived.

It's getting me, he thought—it's getting me at last. He'd seen it happen before, and always admitted that it might happen to him—but it was a shock.

Hesitantly, which was strange for him, he asked if he could somehow find his way across the desert to Portsmouth. The creature ticked approvingly, brought in sand and with one delicate appendage began to trace what might be a map.

He was going to do it. He was going to be clean again, he who had always had a horror of filth and never until now had seen that his life was viler than maggots, more loathesome than carrion. A warm glow of self-approval filled him while he bent over the map. Yes, he was going to perform the incredible hike and somehow make restitution to her. Who would have thought an inhuman creature like his benefactor could have done this to him? With all the enthusiasm of any convert, he felt young again, with life before him, a life where he could choose between fair and foul. He chuckled with the newness of it.

But to work! Good intentions were not enough. There was the map to memorize, his bearings to establish, some portable food supply to be gathered—

He followed the map with his finger. The tracing appendage of the creature guided him, another quietly lay around him, its tip at the small of his back. He accepted it, though it itched somewhat. Not for an itch would he risk offending the bearer of his new life.

He was going to get Amy to a cure, give her money, bear her abuse—she could not understand all at once that he was another man—turn his undoubted talent to an honest—

Farewell! Farewell!
Farewell, little ones. Farewell.

The map blurred a bit before Smith's eyes. Then the map toppled and slid and became the red-lit ceiling of the burrow. Then Smith tried to move and could not. The itching in his back was a torment.

The screy mother did not look at the prostrate host as she turned and crawled up from the incubator to the surface. Something like fond humor wrinkled the surface of her thoughts as she remembered the little ones and their impatience. Heigh-ho! She had given them the best she could, letting many a smaller host go by until this fine, big host came her way. It had taken feeding and humoring, but it would last many and many a month while the little wrigglers grew and ate and grew within it. Heigh-ho! Life went on, she thought; one did the best one could. . . .

With These Hands

I

HALVORSEN waited in the Chancery office while Monsignor Reedy disposed of three persons who had preceded him. He was a little dizzy with hunger and noticed only vaguely that the prelate's secretary was beckoning to him. He started to his feet when the secretary pointedly opened the door to Monsignor Reedy's inner office and stood waiting beside it.

The artist crossed the floor, forgetting that he had leaned his portfolio against his chair, remembered at the door and went back for it, flushing. The secretary looked patient.

"Thanks," Halvorsen murmured to him as the door closed. There was something wrong with the prelate's manner.

"I've brought the designs for the Stations, Padre," he said, opening the portfolio on the desk.

"Bad news, Roald," said the monsignor. "I know how you've been looking forward to the commission—"

"Somebody else get it?" asked the artist faintly, leaning against the desk. "I thought his eminence definitely decided I had the—"

"It's not that," said the monsignor. "But the Sacred Congregation of Rites this week made a pronouncement on images of devotion. Stereopantograph is to be licit within a diocese at the discretion of the bishop. And his eminence—"

"S.P.G.—slimy imitations," protested Halvorsen. "Real as a plastic eye. No texture. No guts. *You* know that, Padre!" he said accusingly.

"I'm sorry, Roald," said the monsignor. "Your work is better than we'll get from a stereopantograph—to my eyes, at least. But there are other considerations."

"Money!" spat the artist.

"Yes, money," the prelate admitted. "His eminence wants to

97

see the St. Xavier U. building program through before he
dies. Is that wrong, Roald? And there are our schools, our
charities, our Venus mission. S.P.G. will mean a considerable
saving on procurement and maintenance of devotional images.
Even if I could, I would not disagree with his eminence on
adopting it as a matter of diocesan policy."

The prelate's eyes fell on the detailed drawings of the
Stations of the Cross and lingered.

"Your St. Veronica," he said abstractedly. "Very fine. It
suggests one of Caravaggio's careworn saints to me. I would
have liked to see her in the bronze."

"So would I," said Halvorsen hoarsely. "Keep the drawings, Padre." He started for the door.

"But I can't—"

"That's all right."

The artist walked past the secretary blindly and out of the
Chancery into Fifth Avenue's spring sunlight. He hoped
Monsignor Reedy was enjoying the drawings and was ashamed
of himself and sorry for Halvorsen. And he was glad he
didn't have to carry the heavy portfolio any more. Everything
was heavy lately—chisels, hammer, wooden palette. Maybe
the padre would send him something and pretend it was
for expenses or an advance, as he had in the past.

Halvorsen's feet carried him up the Avenue. No, there
wouldn't be any advances any more. The last steady trickle
of income had just been dried up, by an announcement in
Osservatore Romano. Religious conservatism had carried the
church as far as it would go in its ancient role of art patron.

When all Europe was writing on the wonderful new vellum,
the church stuck to good old papyrus. When all Europe was
writing on the wonderful new paper, the church stuck to good
old vellum. When all architects and municipal monument
committees and portrait bust clients were patronizing the
stereopantograph, the church stuck to good old expensive
sculpture. But not any more.

He was passing an S.P.G. salon now, where one of his
Tuesday night pupils worked: one of the few men in the
classes. Mostly they consisted of lazy, moody, irritable girls.
Halvorsen, surprised at himself, entered the salon, walking
between asthenic semi-nude stereos executed in transparent
plastic that made the skin of his neck and shoulders prickle
with gooseflesh.

Slime! he thought. *How can they—*

"May I help—oh, hello, Roald. What brings you here?"

He knew suddenly what had brought him there. "Could you make a little advance on next month's tuition, Lewis? I'm strapped." He took a nervous look around the chamber of horrors, avoiding the man's condescending face.

"I guess so, Roald. Would ten dollars be any help? That'll carry us through to the 25th, right?"

"Fine, right, sure," he said, while he was being unwillingly towed around the place.

"I know you don't think much of ⌐.P.G., but it's quiet now, so this is a good chance to see how we work. I don't say it's Art with a capital A, but you've got to admit it's *an* art, something people like at a price they can afford to pay. Here's where we sit them. Then you run out the feelers to the reference points on the face. You know what they are?"

He heard himself say dryly: "I know what they are. The Egyptian sculptors used them when they carved statues of the pharaohs."

"Yes? I never knew that. There's nothing new under the Sun, is there? But *this* is the heart of the S.P.G." The youngster proudly swung open the door of an electronic device in the wall of the portrait booth. Tubes winked sullenly at Halvorsen.

"The esthetikon?" he asked indifferently. He did not feel indifferent, but it would be absurd to show anger, no matter how much he felt it, against a mindless aggregation of circuits that could calculate layouts, criticize and correct pictures for a desired effect—and that had put the artist of design out of a job.

"Yes. The lenses take sixteen profiles, you know, and we set the esthetikon for whatever we want—cute, rugged, sexy, spiritual, brainy, or a combination. It fairs curves from profile to profile to give us just what we want, distorts the profiles themselves within limits if it has to, and there's your portrait stored in the memory tank waiting to be taped. You set your ratio for any enlargement or reduction you want and play it back. I wish we were reproducing today; it's fascinating to watch. You just pour in your cold-set plastic, the nozzles ooze out a core and start crawling over to scan—a drop here, a worm there, and it begins to take shape.

"We mostly do portrait busts here, the Avenue trade, but Wilgus, the foreman, used to work in a monument shop in

Brooklyn. He did that heroic-size war memorial on the East River Drive—hired Garda Bouchette, the TV girl, for the central figure. And what a figure! He told me he set the esthetikon plates for three-quarter sexy, one-quarter spiritual. Here's something interesting—standing figurine of Orin Ryerson, the banker. He ordered twelve. Figurines are coming in. The girls like them because they can show their shapes. You'd be surprised at some of the poses they want to try—"

Somehow, Halvorsen got out with the ten dollars, walked to Sixth Avenue and sat down hard in a cheap restaurant. He had coffee and dozed a little, waking with a guilty start at a racket across the street. There was a building going up. For a while he watched the great machines pour walls and floors, the workmen rolling here and there on their little chariots to weld on a wall panel, stripe on an electric circuit of conductive ink, or spray plastic finish over the "wired" wall, all without leaving the saddles of their little mechanical chariots.

Halvorsen felt more determined. He bought a paper from a vending machine by the restaurant door, drew another cup of coffee and turned to the help-wanted ads.

The tricky trade-school ads urged him to learn construction work and make big money. Be a plumbing-machine setup man. Be a house-wiring machine tender. Be a servotruck driver. Be a lumber-stacker operator. Learn pouring-machine maintenance.

Make big money!

A sort of panic overcame him. He ran to the phone booth and dialed a Passaic number. He heard the *ring-ring-ring* and strained to hear old Mr. Krehbeil's stumping footsteps growing louder as he neared the phone, even though he knew he would hear nothing until the receiver was picked up.

Ring-ring-ring. "Hello?" grunted the old man's voice, and his face appeared on the little screen. "Hello, Mr. Halvorsen. What can I do for you?"

Halvorsen was tongue-tied. He couldn't possibly say: I just wanted to see if you were still there. I was afraid you weren't there any more. He choked and improvised: "Hello, Mr. Krehbeil. It's about the banister on the stairs in my place. I noticed it's pretty shaky. Could you come over sometime and fix it for me?"

Krehbeil peered suspiciously out of the screen. "I could

do that," he said slowly. "I don't have much work nowadays. But you can carpenter as good as me, Mr. Halvorsen, and frankly you're very slow pay and I like cabinet work better. I'm not a young man and climbing around on ladders takes it out of me. If you can't find anybody else, I'll take the work, but I got to have some of the money first, just for the materials. It isn't easy to get good wood any more."

"All right," said Halvorsen. "Thanks, Mr. Krehbeil. I'll call you if I can't get anybody else."

He hung up and went back to his table and newspaper. His face was burning with anger at the old man's reluctance and his own foolish panic. Krehbeil didn't realize they were both in the same leaky boat. Krehbeil, who didn't get a job in a month, still thought with senile pride that he was a journeyman carpenter and cabinetmaker who could make his solid way anywhere with his toolbox and his skill, and that he could afford to look down on anything as disreputable as an artist—even an artist who could carpenter as well as he did himself.

Labeurre had made Halvorsen learn carpentry, and Labeurre had been right. You build a scaffold so you can sculp up high, not so it will collapse and you break a leg. You build your platforms so they hold the rock steady, not so it wobbles and chatters at every blow of the chisel. You build your armatures so they hold the plasticine you slam onto them.

But the help-wanted ads wanted no builders of scaffolds, platforms and armatures. The factories were calling for set-up men and maintenance men for the production and assembly machines.

From upstate, General Vegetables had sent a recruiting team for farm help—harvest setup and maintenance men, a few openings for experienced operators of tankcaulking machinery. Under "office and professional" the demand was heavy for computer men, for girls who could run the I.B.M. Letteriter, esp. familiar sales and collections corresp., for office machinery maintenance and repair men. A job printing house wanted an esthetikon operator for letterhead layouts and the like. A.T. & T. wanted trainees to earn while learning telephone maintenance. A direct-mail advertising outfit wanted an artist—no, they wanted a sales-executive who could scrawl picture-ideas that would be subjected to the criticism and correction of the esthetikon.

Halvorsen leafed tiredly through the rest of the paper. He knew he wouldn't get a job, and if he did he wouldn't hold it. He knew it was a terrible thing to admit to yourself that you might starve to death because you were bored by anything except art, but he admitted it.

It had happened often enough in the past—artists undergoing preposterous hardships, not, as people thought, because they were devoted to art, but because nothing else was interesting. If there were only some impressive, sonorous word that summed up the aching, oppressive futility that overcame him when he tried to get out of art—only there wasn't.

He thought he could tell which of the photos in the tabloid had been corrected by the esthetikon.

There was a shot of Jink Bitsy, who was to star in a remake of *Peter Pan*. Her ears had been made to look not pointed but pointy, her upper lip had been lengthened a trifle, her nose had been pugged a little and tilted quite a lot, her freckles were cuter than cute, her brows were innocently arched, and her lower lip and eyes were nothing less than pornography.

There was a shot, apparently uncorrected, of the last Venus ship coming in at La Guardia and the average-looking explorers grinning. Caption: "Austin Malone and crew smile relief on safe arrival. Malone says Venus colonies need men, machines. See story on p. 2."

Petulantly, Halvorsen threw the paper under the table and walked out. What had space travel to do with him? Vacations on the Moon and expeditions to Venus and Mars were part of the deadly encroachment on his livelihood and no more.

II

He took the subway to Passaic and walked down a long-still traffic beltway to his studio, almost the only building alive in the slums near the rusting railroad freightyard.

A sign that had once said "F. Labuerre, Sculptor—Portraits and Architectural Commissions" now said "Roald Halvorsen;

Art Classes—Reasonable Fees." It was a grimy two-story frame building with a shopfront in which were mounted some of his students' charcoal figure studies and oil still-lifes. He lived upstairs, taught downstairs front, and did his own work downstairs, back behind dirty, ceiling-high drapes.

Going in, he noticed that he had forgotten to lock the door again. He slammed it bitterly. At the noise, somebody called from behind the drapes: "Who's that?"

"Halvorsen!" he yelled in a sudden fury. "I live here. I own this place. Come out of there! What do you want?"

There was a fumbling at the drapes and a girl stepped between them, shrinking from their dirt.

"Your door was open," she said firmly, "and it's a shop. I've just been here a couple of minutes. I came to ask about classes, but I don't think I'm interested if you're this bad-tempered."

A pupil. Pupils were never to be abused, especially not now. "I'm terribly sorry," he said. "I had a trying day in the city." Now turn it on. "I wouldn't tell everybody a terrible secret like this, but I've lost a commission. You understand? I thought so. Anybody who'd traipse out here to my dingy abode would be *simpatica*. Won't you sit down? No, not there —humor an artist and sit over there. The warm background of that still-life brings out your color—quite good color. Have you ever been painted? You've a very interesting face, you know. Some day I'd like to—but you mentioned classes.

"We have figure classes, male and female models alternating, on Tuesday nights. For that I have to be very stern and ask you to sign up for an entire course of twelve lessons at sixty dollars. It's the models' fees—they're exorbitant. Saturday afternoons we have still-life classes for beginners in oils. That's only two dollars a class, but you might sign up for a series of six and pay ten dollars in advance, which saves you two whole dollars. I also give private instructions to a few talented amateurs."

The price was open on that one—whatever the traffic would bear. It had been a year since he'd had a private pupil and she'd taken only six lessons at five dollars an hour.

"The still-life sounds interesting," said the girl, holding her head self-consciously the way they all did when he gave them the patter. It was a good head, carried well up. The muscles clung close, not yet slacked into geotropic loops and lumps. The line of youth is heliotropic, he confusedly thought. "I saw some interesting things back there. Was that your own work?"

She rose, obviously with the expectation of being taken into the studio. Her body was one of those long-lined, small-breasted, coltish jobs that the pre-Raphaelites loved to draw.

"Well—' said Halvorsen. A deliberate show of reluctance and then a bright smile of confidence. "*You'll* understand," he said positively and drew aside the curtains.

"What a curious place!" She wandered about, inspecting the drums of plaster, clay and plasticene, the racks of tools, the stands, the stones, the chisels, the forge, the kiln, the lumber, the glaze bench.

"I *like* this," she said determinedly, picking up a figure a half-meter tall, a Venus he had cast in bronze while studying under Labuerre some years ago. "How much is it?"

An honest answer would scare her off, and there was no chance in the world that she'd buy. "I hardly ever put my things up for sale," he told her lightly. "That was just a little study. I do work on commission only nowadays."

Her eyes flicked about the dingy room, seeming to take in its scaling plaster and warped floor and see through the wall to the abandoned slum in which it was set. There was amusement in her glance.

I am not being honest, she thinks. She thinks that is funny. Very well, I will be honest. "Six hundred dollars," he said flatly.

The girl set the figurine on its stand with a rap and said, half angry and half amused: "I don't understand it. That's more than a month's pay for me. I could get an S.P.G. statuette just as pretty as this for ten dollars. Who do you artists think you are, anyway?"

Halvorsen debated with himself about what he could say in reply:

An S.P.G. operator spends a week learning his skill and I spend a lifetime learning mine.

An S.P.G. operator makes a mechanical copy of a human form distorted by formulae mechanically arrived at from psychotests of population samples. I take full responsibility for my work; it is mine, though I use what I see fit from Egypt, Greece, Rome, the Middle Ages, the Renaissance, the Augustan and Romantic and Modern Eras.

An S.P.G. operator works in soft, homogeneous plastic; I

*work in bronze that is more complicated than you dream, that
is cast and acid-dipped today so it will slowly take on rich and
subtle coloring many years from today.*

An S.P.G. operator could not make an Orpheus Fountain—
He mumbled, "Orpheus," and keeled over.

Halvorsen awoke in his bed on the second floor of the
building. His fingers and toes buzzed electrically and he felt
very clear-headed. The girl and a man, unmistakably a doctor,
were watching him.

"You don't seem to belong to any Medical Plans, Halvorsen," the doctor said irritably. "There weren't any cards on
you at all. No Red, no Blue, no Green, no Brown."

"I used to be on the Green Plan, but I let it lapse," the
artist said defensively.

"And look what happened!"

"Stop nagging him!" the girl said. "I'll pay you your fee."

"It's supposed to come through a Plan," the doctor fretted.

"We won't tell anybody," the girl promised. "Here's five
dollars. Just stop nagging him."

"Malnutrition," said the doctor. "Normally I'd send him to
a hospital, but I don't see how I could manage it. He isn't
on any Plan at all. Look, I'll take the money and leave some
vitamins. That's what he needs—vitamins. And food."

"I'll see that he eats," the girl said, and the doctor left.

"How long since you've had anything?" she asked Halvorsen.

"I had some coffee today," he answered, thinking back. "I'd
been working on detail drawings for a commission and it fell
through. I told you that. It was a shock."

"I'm Lucretia Grumman," she said, and went out.

He dozed until she came back with an armful of groceries.

"It's hard to get around down here," she complained.

"It was Labuerre's studio," he told her defiantly. "He left it
to me when he died. Things weren't so rundown in his time.
I studied under him; he was one of the last. He had a joke—
'They don't really want my stuff, but they're ashamed to let
me starve.' He warned me that they wouldn't be ashamed to
let *me* starve, but I insisted and he took me in."

Halvorsen drank some milk and ate some bread. He thought
of the change from the ten dollars in his pocket and decided

not to mention it. Then he remembered that the doctor had gone through his pockets.

"I can pay you for this," he said. "It's very kind of you, but you mustn't think I'm penniless. I've just been too preoccupied to take care of myself."

"Sure," said the girl. "But we can call this an advance. I want to sign up for some classes."

"Be happy to have you."

"Am I bothering you?" asked the girl. "You said something odd when you fainted—'Orpheus.' "

"Did I say that? I must have been thinking of Milles' Orpheus Fountain in Copenhagen. I've seen photos, but I've never been there."

"Germany? But there's nothing left of Germany."

"Copenhagen's in Denmark. There's quite a lot of Denmark left. It was only on the fringes. Heavily radiated, but still there."

"I want to travel, too," she said. "I work at La Guardia and I've never been off, except for an orbiting excursion. I want to go to the Moon on my vacation. They give us a bonus in travel vouchers. It must be wonderful dancing under the low gravity."

Spaceport? Off? Low gravity? Terms belonging to the detested electronic world of the stereopantograph in which he had no place.

"Be very interesting," he said, closing his eyes to conceal disgust.

"I *am* bothering you. I'll go away now, but I'll be back Tuesday night for the class. What time do I come and what should I bring?"

"Eight. It's charcoal—I sell you the sticks and paper. Just bring a smock."

"All right. And I want to take the oils class, too. And I want to bring some people I know to see your work. I'm sure they'll see something they like. Austin Malone's in from Venus—he's a special friend of mine."

"Lucretia," he said. "Or do some people call you Lucy?"

"Lucy."

"Will you take that little bronze you liked? As a thank you?"

"I can't do that!"

"Please. I'd feel much better about this. I really mean it."

She nodded abruptly, flushing, and almost ran from the room.

Now why did I do that? he asked himself. He hoped it was because he liked Lucy Grumman very much. He hoped it wasn't a cold-blooded investment of a piece of sculpture that would never be sold, anyway, just to make sure she'd be back with class fees and more groceries.

III

She was back on Tuesday, a half-hour early and carrying a smock. He introduced her formally to the others as they arrived: a dozen or so bored young women who, he suspected, talked a great deal about their art lessons outside, but in class used any excuse to stop sketching.

He didn't dare show Lucy any particular consideration. There were fierce little miniature cliques in the class. Halvorsen knew they laughed at him and his line among themselves, and yet, strangely, were fiercely jealous of their seniority and right to individual attention.

The lesson was an ordeal, as usual. The model, a muscle-bound young graduate of the barbell gyms and figure-photography studios, was stupid and argumentative about ten-minute poses. Two of the girls came near a hair-pulling brawl over the rights to a preferred sketching location. A third girl had discovered Picasso's cubist period during the past week and proudly announced that she didn't *feel* perspective.

But the two interminable hours finally ticked by. He nagged them into cleaning up—not as bad as the Saturdays with oils—and stood by the open door. Otherwise they would have stayed all night, cackling about absent students and snarling sulkily among themselves. His well-laid plans went sour, though. A large and flashy car drove up as the girls were leaving.

"That's Austin Malone," said Lucy. "He came to pick me up and look at your work."

That was all the wedge her fellow-pupils needed.

"*Aus*-tin Ma-*lone! Well!*"

"Lucy, darling, I'd love to meet a real *spaceman*."

"Roald, darling, would you mind very much if I stayed a moment?"

"I'm certainly not going to miss this and I don't care if you mind or not, Roald, darling!"

Malone was an impressive figure. Halvorsen thought: he looks as though he's been run through an esthetikon set for 'brawny' and 'determined.' Lucy made a hash of the introductions and the spaceman didn't rise to conversational bait dangled enticingly by the girls.

In a clear voice, he said to Halvorsen: "I don't want to take up too much of your time. Lucy tells me you have some things for sale. Is there any place we can look at them where it's quiet?"

The students made sulky exits.

"Back here," said the artist.

The girl and Malone followed him through the curtains. The spaceman made a slow circuit of the studio, seeming to repel questions.

He sat down at last and said: "I don't know what to think, Halvorsen. This place stuns me. Do you *know* you're in the Dark Ages?"

People who never have given a thought to Chartres and Mont St. Michel usually call it the Dark Ages, Halvorsen thought wryly. He asked, "Technologically, you mean? No, not at all. My plaster's better, my colors are better, my metal is better—tool metal, not casting metal, that is."

"I mean *hand* work;" said the spaceman. "Actually working by *hand*."

The artist shrugged. "There have been crazes for the techniques of the boiler works and the machine shop," he admitted. "Some interesting things were done, but they didn't stand up well. Is there anything here that takes your eye?"

"I like those dolphins," said the spaceman, pointing to a perforated terra-cotta relief on the wall. They had been commissioned by an architect, then later refused for reasons of economy when the house had run way over estimate. "They'd look bully over the fireplace in my town apartment. Like them, Lucy?"

"I think they're wonderful," said the girl.

Roald saw the spaceman go rigid with the effort not to turn and stare at her. He loved her and he was jealous.

Roald told the story of the dolphins and said: "The price

that the architect thought was too high was three hundred and sixty dollars."

Malone grunted. "Doesn't seem unreasonable—if you set a high store on inspiration."

"I don't know about inspiration," the artist said evenly. "But I was awake for two days and two nights shoveling coal and adjusting drafts to fire that thing in my kiln."

The spaceman looked contemptuous. "I'll take it," he said. "Be something to talk about during those awkward pauses. Tell me, Halvorsen, how's Lucy's work? Do you think she ought to stick with it?"

"Austin," objected the girl, "don't be so blunt. How can he possibly know after one day?"

"She can't draw yet," the artist said cautiously. "It's all coordination, you know—thousands of hours of practice, training your eye and hand to work together until you can put a line on paper where you want it. Lucy, if you're really interested in it, you'll learn to draw well. I don't think any of the other students will. They're in it because of boredom or snobbery, and they'll stop before they have their eye-hand coordination."

"I *am* interested," she said firmly.

Malone's determined restraint broke. "Damned right you are. In—" He recovered himself and demanded of Halvorsen: "I understand your point about coordination. But thousands of hours when you can buy a camera? It's absurd."

"I was talking about drawing, not art," replied Halvorsen. "Drawing is putting a line on paper where you want it, I said." He took a deep breath and hoped the great distinction wouldn't sound ludicrous and trivial. "So let's say that art is knowing how to put the line in the right place."

"Be practical. There isn't any art. Not any more. I get around quite a bit and I never see anything but photos and S.P.G.s. A few heirlooms, yes, but nobody's painting or carving any more."

"There's some art, Malone. My students—a couple of them in the still-life class—are quite good. There are more across the country. Art for occupational therapy, or a hobby, or something to do with the hands. There's trade in their work. They sell them to each other, they give them to their friends, they hang them on their walls. There are even some sculptors like that. Sculpture is prescribed by doctors. The occupational therapists say it's even better than drawing and painting, so some of these people work in plasticene and soft stone, and some of them get to be good."

"Maybe so. I'm an engineer, Halvorsen. We glory in doing things the easy way. Doing things the easy way got me to Mars and Venus and it's going to get me to Ganymede. You're doing things the hard way, and your inefficiency has no place in this world. Look at you! You've lost a fingertip—some accident, I suppose."

"I never noticed—" said Lucy, and then let out a faint, "Oh!"

Halvorsen curled the middle finger of his left hand into the palm, where he usually carried it to hide the missing first joint.

"Accidents are a sign of inadequate mastery of material and equipment," said Malone sententiously. "While you stick to your methods and I stick to mine, *you can't compete with me.*"

His tone made it clear that he was talking about more than engineering.

"Shall we go now, Lucy? Here's my card, Halvorsen. Send those dolphins along and I'll mail you a check."

IV

The artist walked the half-dozen blocks to Mr. Krehbeil's place the next day. He found the old man in the basement shop of his fussy house, hunched over his bench with a powerful light overhead. He was trying to file a saw.

"Mr. Krehbeil!" Halvorsen called over the shriek of metal.

The carpenter turned around and peered with watery eyes. "I can't see like I used to," he said querulously. "I go over the same teeth on this damn saw, I skip teeth, I can't see the light shine off it when I got one set. The glare." He banged down his three-cornered file petulantly. "Well, what can I do for you?"

"I need some crating stock. Anything. I'll trade you a couple of my maple four-by-fours."

The old face became cunning. "And will you set my saw?

My *saws*, I mean. It's nothing to you—an hour's work. You have the eyes."

Halvorsen said bitterly. "All right." The old man had to drive his bargain, even though he might never use his saws again. And then the artist promptly repented of his bitterness, offering up a quick prayer that his own failure to conform didn't make him as much of a nuisance to the world as Krehbeil was.

The carpenter was pleased as they went through his small stock of wood and chose boards to crate the dolphin relief. He was pleased enough to give Halvorsen coffee and cake before the artist buckled down to filing the saws.

Over the kitchen table, Halvorsen tried to probe. "Things pretty slow now?"

It would be hard to spoil Krehbeil's day now. "People are always fools. They don't know good hand work. Some day," he said apocalyptically, "I laugh on the other side of my face when their foolish machine-buildings go falling down in a strong wind, all of them, all over the country. Even my boy—I used to beat him good, almost every day—he works a foolish concrete machine and his house should fall on his head like the rest."

Halvorsen knew it was Krehbeil's son who supported him by mail, and changed the subject. "You get some cabinet work?"

"Stupid women! What they call antiques—they don't know Meissen, they don't know Biedermeier. They bring me trash to repair sometimes. I make them pay; I swindle them good."

"I wonder if things would be different if there were anything left over in Europe . . ."

"People will still be fools, Mr. Halvorsen," said the carpenter positively. "Didn't you say you were going to file those saws today?"

So the artist spent two noisy hours filing before he carried his crating stock to the studio.

Lucy was there. She had brought some things to eat. He dumped the lumber with a bang and demanded: "Why aren't you at work?"

"We get days off," she said vaguely. "Austin thought he'd give me the cash for the terra-cotta and I could give it to you."

She held out an envelope while he studied her silently. The farce was beginning again. But this time he dreaded it.

It would not be the first time that a lonesome, discontented girl chose to see him as a combination of romantic rebel and lost pup, with the consequences you'd expect.

He knew from books, experience and Labuerre's conversation in the old days that there was nothing novel about the comedy—that there had even been artists, lots of them, who had counted on endless repetitions of it for their livelihood.

The girl drops in with groceries and the artist is pleasantly surprised; the girl admires this little thing or that after payday and buys it and the artist is pleasantly surprised; the girl brings her friends to take lessons or make little purchases and the artist is pleasantly surprised. The girl may be seduced by the artist or vice versa, which shortens the comedy, or they may get married, which lengthens it somewhat.

It had been three years since Halvorsen had last played out the farce with a manic-depressive divorcee from Elmira: three years during which he had crossed the mid-point between thirty and forty; three more years to get beaten down by being unwanted and working too much and eating too little.

Also, he knew, he was in love with this girl.

He took the envelope, counted three hundred and twenty dollars and crammed it into his pocket. "That was your idea," he said. "Thanks. Now get out, will you? I've got work to do."

She stood there, shocked.

"I said get out. I have work to do."

"Austin was right," she told him miserably. "You don't care how people feel. You just want to get things out of them."

She ran from the studio, and Halvorsen fought with himself not to run after her.

He walked slowly into his workshop and studied his array of tools, though he paid little attention to his finished pieces. It would be nice to spend about half of this money on open-hearth steel rod and bar stock to forge into chisels; he thought he knew where he could get some—but she would be back, or he would break and go to her and be forgiven and the comedy would be played out, after all.

He couldn't let that happen.

V

Aalesund, on the Atlantic side of the Dourefeld mountains of Norway, was in the lee of the blasted continent. One more archeologist there made no difference, as long as he had the sense to recognize the propellor-like international sign-posts that said with their three blades, *Radiation Hazard,* and knew what every schoolboy knew about protective clothing and reading a personal Geiger counter.

The car Halvorsen rented was for a brief trip over the mountains to study contaminated Oslo. Well-muffled, he could make it and back in a dozen hours and no harm done.

But he took the car past Oslo, Wennersborg and Goteborg, along the Kattegat coast to Helsingborg, and abandoned it there, among the three-bladed polyglot signs, crossing to Denmark. Danes were as unlike Prussians as they could be, but their unfortunate little peninsula was a sprout off Prussia which radio-cobalt dust couldn't tell from the real thing. The three-bladed signs were most specific.

With a long way to walk along the rubble-littered highways, he stripped off the impregnated coveralls and boots. He had long since shed the noisy counter and the uncomfortable gloves and mask.

The silence was eerie as he limped into Copenhagen at noon. He didn't know whether the radiation was getting to him or whether he was tired and hungry and no more. As though thinking of a stranger, he liked what he was doing.

I'll be my own audience, he thought. God knows I learned there isn't any other, not any more. You have to know when to stop. Rodin, the dirty old, wonderful old man, knew that. He taught us not to slick it and polish it and smooth it until it looked like liquid instead of bronze and stone. Van Gogh was crazy as a loon, but he knew when to stop and varnish it, and he didn't care if the paint looked like paint instead of look-ing like sunset clouds or moonbeams. Up in Hartford, Browne and Sharpe stop when they've got a turret lathe; they don't put caryatids on it. I'll stop while my life is a life, before it becomes a thing with distracting embellishments such as a wife who will come to despise me, a succession of gradu-ally less worthwhile pieces that nobody will look at.

Blame nobody, he told himself, lightheadedly.

And then it was in front of him, terminating a vista of weeds and bomb rubble—Milles' Orpheus Fountain.

It took a man, he thought. Esthetikon circuits couldn't do it. There was a gross mixture of styles, a calculated flaw that the esthetikon couldn't be set to make. Orpheus and the souls were classic or later; the three-headed dog was archaic. That was to tell you about the antiquity and invincibility of Hell, and that Cerberus knows Orpheus will never go back into life with his bride. ·

There was the heroic, tragic central figure that looked mighty enough to battle with the gods, but battle wasn't any good against the grinning, knowing, hateful three-headed dog it stood on. You don't battle the pavement where you walk or the floor of the house you're in; you can't. So Orpheus, his face a mask of controlled and suffering fury, crashes a great chord from his lyre that moved trees and stones. Around him the naked souls in Hell start at the chord, each in its own way: the young lovers down in death; the mother down in death; the musician, deaf and down in death, straining to hear.

Halvorsen, walking uncertainly toward the fountain, felt something break inside him, and a heaviness in his lungs. As he pitched forward among the weeds, he didn't care that the three-headed dog was grinning its knowing, hateful grin down at him. He had heard the chord from the lyre.

That Share of Glory

YOUNG ALEN, one of a thousand in the huge refectory, ate absent-mindedly as the reader droned into the perfect silence of the hall. Today's lesson happened to be a word-list of the Thetis VIII planet's sea-going folk.

"*Tlon*—a ship," droned the reader.

"*Rtlo*—some ships, number unknown.

"*Long*—some ships, number known, always modified by cardinal.

"*Ongr*—a ship in a collection of ships, always modified by ordinal.

"*Ngrt*—first ship in a collection of ships; an exception to *ongr*."

A lay brother tiptoed to Alen's side. "The Rector summons you," he whispered.

Alen had no time for panic, though that was the usual reaction to a summons from the Rector to a novice. He slipped from the refectory, stepped onto the northbound corridor and stepped off at his cell, a minute later and a quarter-mile farther on. Hastily, but meticulously, he changed from his drab habit to the heraldic robes in the cubicle with its simple stool, washstand, desk, and paperweight or two. Alen, a level-headed young fellow, was not aware that he had broken any section of the Order's complicated Rule, but he was aware that he could have done so without knowing it. It might, he thought, be the last time he would see the cell.

He cast a glance which he hoped would not be the final one over it; a glance which lingered a little fondly on the reel rack where were stowed: "Nicholson on Martian Verbs," "The New Oxford Venusian Dictionary," the ponderous sixreeler "Deutche-Ganymediche Konversasionslexikon" published long ago and far away in Leipzig. The later works were there, too: "The Tongues of the Galaxy—An Essay in Classification," "A Concise Grammar of Cephean," "The Self-Pronouncing Vegan II Dictionary"—scores of them, and, of course, the worn reel of old Machiavelli's "The Prince."

Enough of that! Alen combed out his small, neat beard and stepped onto the southbound corridor. He transferred to an eastbound at the next intersection and minutes later was before the Rector's lay secretary.

"You'd better review your Lyran irregulars," said the secretary disrespectfully. "There's a trader in there who's looking for a cheap herald on a swindling trip to Lyra VI." Thus unceremoniously did Alen learn that he was not to be ejected from the Order but that he was to be elevated to Journeyman. But as a herald should, he betrayed no sign of his immense relief. He did, however, take the secretary's advice and sensibly reviewed his Lyran.

While he was in the midst of a declension which applied only to inanimate objects, the voice of the Rector—and what a mellow voice it was!—floated through the secretary's intercom.

"Admit the novice, Alen," said the Master Herald.

A final settling of his robes and the youth walked into the Rector's huge office, with the seal of the Order blazing in diamonds above his desk. There was a stranger present; presumably the trader—a black-bearded fellow whose rugged frame didn't carry his Vegan cloak with ease.

Said the Rector: "Novice, this is to be the crown of your toil if you are acceptable to—?" He courteously turned to the trader, who shrugged irritably.

"It's all one to me," growled the blackbeard. "Somebody cheap, somebody who knows the cant of the thievish Lyran gem peddlers, above all, somebody *at once*. Overhead is devouring my flesh day by day as the ship waits at the field. And when we are space-borne, my imbecile crew will doubtless waste liter after priceless liter of my fuel. And when we land the swindling Lyrans will without doubt make my ruin complete by tricking me even out of the minute profit I hope to realize. Good Master Herald, let me have the infant cheap and I'll bid you good day."

The Rector's shaggy eyebrows drew down in a frown. "Trader," he said sonorously, "our mission of galactic utilitarian culture is not concerned with your margin of profit. I ask you to test this youth and, if you find him able, to take him as your Herald on your voyage. He will serve you well, for he has been taught that commerce and words, its medium, are the unifying bonds which will one day unite the cosmos into a single humankind. Do not conceive that the College and Order of Heralds is a mere aid to you in your commercial adventure."

"Very well," growled the trader. He addressed Alen in broken Lyran: "Boy, how you make up Vegan stones of three fires so Lyran women like, come buy, buy again?"

Alen smoothly replied: "The Vegan triple-fire gem finds most favor on Lyran and especially among its women when set in a wide glass anklet if large, and when arranged in the Lyran 'lucky five' pattern in a glass thumb-ring if small." He was glad, very glad, he had come across—and as a matter of course memorized, in the relentless fashion of the Order—a novel which touched briefly on the Lyran jewel trade.

The trader glowered and switched to Cephean—apparently his native tongue. "That was well-enough said, Herald. Now tell me whether you've got guts to man a squirt in case we're intercepted by the thieving so-called Customs collectors of Eyolf's Realm between here and Lyra?"

Alen knew the Rector's eyes were on him. "The noble mission of our Order," he said, "forbids me to use any weapon but the truth in furthering cosmic utilitarian civilization. No, master trader, I shall not man one of your weapons."

The trader shrugged. "So I must take what I get. Good Master Herald, make me a price."

The Rector said casually: "I regard this chiefly as a training mission for our novice; the fee will be nominal. Let us say twenty-five per cent of your net as of blastoff from Lyra, to be audited by Journeyman-Herald Alen."

The trader's howl of rage echoed in the dome of the huge room. "It's not fair!" he roared. "Who but you thievish villains with your Order and your catch-'em-young and your years of training can learn the tongues of the galaxy? What chance has a decent merchant busy with profit and loss got to learn the cant of every race between Sirius and the Coalsack? It's not fair! It's not fair and I'll say so until my dying breath!"

"Die outside if you find our terms unacceptable," said the Rector. "The Order does not haggle."

"Well I know it," sighed the trader brokenly. "I should have stuck to my own system and my good father's pump-flange factory. But no! I had to pick up a bargain in gems on Vego! Enough of this—bring me your contract and I'll sign it."

The Rector's shaggy eyebrows went up. "There is no contract," he said. "A mutual trust between Herald and trader is the cornerstone upon which cosmos-wide amity and understanding will be built."

"At twenty-five per cent for an unlicked pup," muttered blackbeard to himself in Cephean.

None of his instructors had played Polonius as Alen, with the seal of the Journeyman-Herald on his brow, packed for blastoff and vacated his cell. He supposed they knew that twenty years of training either had done their work or had not.

The trader taking Alen to the field where his ship waited, was less wise. "The secret of successful negotiation," he weightily told his Herald, "is to yield willingly. This may strike you as a paradox, but it is the veritable key to my success in maintaining the profits of my good father's pump-flange trade. The secret is to yield with rueful admiration of your opponent—but *only in unimportant details*. Put up a little battle about delivery date or about terms of credit and then let him have his way. But you never give way a hair's breadth on your asking price unless—"

Alen let him drivel on as they drove through the outer works of the College. He was glad the car was open. For the first time he was being accorded the doffed hat that is the due of Heralds from their inferiors in the Order, and the grave nod of salutation from equals. Five-year-old postulants seeing his brow-seal tugged off their headgear with comical celerity; fellow-novices, equals a few hours before, uncovered as though he were the Rector himself.

The ceremonial began to reach the trader. When, with a final salutation, a lay warder let them through the great gate of the curtain wall, he said with some irritation: "They appear to hold you in high regard, boy."

"I am better addressed as 'Herald'," said Alen composedly.

"A plague descend on the College and Order! Do you think I don't know my manners? Of course, I call a Herald 'Herald,' but we're going to be cooped up together and you'll be working for me. What'll happen to ship's discipline if I have to kowtow to you?"

"There will be no problem," said Alen.

Blackbeard grunted and trod fiercely on the accelerator.

"That's my ship," he said at length. "*Starsong*. Vegan registry—it may help passing through Eyolf's Realm, though it cost me overmuch in bribes. A crew of eight, lazy, good-for-nothing wastrels—Agh! Can I believe my eyes?" The car jammed to a halt before the looming ship and blackbeard was up the ladder and through the port in a second. Settling his robes, Alen followed.

He found the trader fiercely denouncing his chief engineer for using space drive to heat the ship; he had seen the faint haze of a minimum exhaust from the stern tubes.

"For that, dolt," screamed blackbeard, "we have a thing known as electricity. Have you by chance ever heard of it? Are you aware that a chief engineer's responsibility is the efficient and *economical* operation of his ship's drive mechanism?"

The chief, a cowed-looking Cephean, saw Alen with relief and swept off his battered cap. The Herald nodded gravely and the trader broke off in irritation. "We need none of that bowing and scraping for the rest of the voyage," he declared.

"Of course not, sir," said the chief. "O'course not. I was just welcoming the Herald aboard. Welcome aboard, Herald. I'm Chief Elwon, Herald. And I'm glad to have a Herald with us." A covert glance at the trader. "*I've* voyaged with Heralds and without, and I don't mind saying I feel safer indeed with you aboard."

"May I be taken to my quarters?" asked Alen.

"Your—?" began the trader, stupefied.

The chief broke in: "I'll fix you a cabin, Herald. We've got some bulkheads I can rig aft for a snug little space, not roomy, but the best a little ship like this can afford."

The trader collapsed into a bucket seat as the chief bustled aft and Alen followed.

"Herald," the chief said with some embarrassment after he had collared two crewmen and set them to work, "you'll have to excuse our good master trader. He's new to the interstar lanes and he doesn't exactly know the jets yet. Between us we'll get him squared away."

Alen inspected the cubicle run up for him—a satisfactory enclosure affording him the decent privacy he rated. He dismissed the chief and the crewmen with a nod and settled himself on the cot.

Beneath the iron composure in which he had been trained, he felt scared and alone. Not even old Machiavelli seemed to offer comfort or council: "There is nothing more difficult to take in hand, more perilous to conduct, or more uncertain in its success, than to take the lead in the introduction of a new order of things," said Chapter Six.

But what said Chapter Twenty-Six? "Where the willingness is great, the difficulties cannot be great."

Starsong was not a happy ship. Blackbeard's nagging stinginess hung over the crew like a thundercloud, but Alen professed not to notice. He walked regularly fore and aft for two hours a day greeting the crew members in their various native tongues and then wrapping himself in the reserve the Order demanded—though he longed to salute them man-to-man, eat with them, gossip about their native planets, the past misdeeds that had brought them to their berths aboard the miserly *Starsong,* their hopes for the future. The Rule of the College and Order of Heralds decreed otherwise. He accepted the uncoverings of the crew with a nod and tried to be pleased because they stood in growing awe of him that ranged from Chief Elwon's lively appreciation of a Herald's skill to Wiper Jukkl's superstitious reverence. Jukkl was a low-browed specimen from a planet of the decadent Sirius system. He outdid the normal slovenliness of an all-male crew on a freighter —a slovenliness in which Alen could not share. Many of his waking hours were spent in his locked cubicle burnishing his metal and cleaning and pressing his robes. A Herald was never supposed to suggest by his appearance that he shared moral frailties.

Blackbeard himself yielded a little, to the point of touching his cap sullenly. This probably was not so much awe at Alen's studied manner as respect for the incisive, lightning-fast job of auditing the Herald did on the books of the trading venture —absurdly complicated books with scores of accounts to record a simple matter of buying gems cheap on Vega and chartering a ship in the hope of selling them dearly on Lyra. The complicated books and overlapping accounts did tell the story, but they made it very easy for an auditor to erroneously read a number of costs as far higher than they actually were. Alen did not fall into the trap.

On the fifth day after blastoff, Chief Elwon rapped, respectfully but urgently, on the door of Alen's cubicle.

"If you please, Herald," he urged, "could you come to the bridge?"

Alen's heart bounded in his chest, but he gravely said: "My meditation must not be interrupted. I shall join you on the bridge in ten minutes." And for ten minutes he methodically polished a murky link in the massive gold chain that fastened his boat-cloak—the "meditation." He donned the cloak before stepping out; the summons sounded like a full-dress affair in the offing.

The trader was stamping and fuming. Chief Elwon was riffling through his spec book unhappily. Astrogator Hufner was at the plot computer running up trajectories and knocking them down again. A quick glance showed Alen that they were all high-speed trajectories in the "evasive action" class.

"Herald," said the trader grimly, "we have broken somebody's detector bubble." He jerked his thumb at a red-lit signal. "I expect we'll be overhauled shortly. Are you ready to earn your twenty-five per cent of the net?"

Alen overlooked the crudity. "Are you rigged for color video, merchant?" he asked.

"We are."

"Then I am ready to do what I can for my client."

He took the communicator's seat, stealing a glance in the still-blank screen. The reflection of his face was reassuring, though he wished he had thought to comb his small beard.

Another light flashed on, and Hufner quit the operator to study the detector board. "Big, powerful and getting closer," he said tersely. "Scanning for us with directionals now. Putting out plenty of energy—"

The loud-speaker of the ship-to-ship audio came to life.

"What ship are you?" it demanded in Vegan. "We are a Customs cruiser of the Realm of Eyolf. What ship are you?"

"Have the crew man the squirts," said the trader softly to the chief.

Elwon looked at Alen, who shook his head. "Sorry, sir," said the engineer apologetically. "The Herald—"

"We are the freighter *Starsong,* Vegan registry," said Alen into the audio mike as the trader choked. "We are carrying Vegan gems to Lyra."

"They're on us," said the astrogator despairingly, reading his instruments. The ship-to-ship video flashed on, showing an arrogant, square-jawed face topped by a battered naval cap.

"Lyra indeed! We have plans of our own for Lyra. You will heave to—" began the officer in the screen, before he noted Alen. "My pardon, Herald," he said sardonically. "Herald, will you please request the ship's master to heave to for boarding and search? We wish to assess and collect Customs duties. You are aware, of course, that your vessel is passing through the Realm."

The man's accented Vegan reeked of Algol IV. Alen switched to that obscure language to say: "We were not aware of that. Are you aware that there is a reciprocal trade treaty in effect between the Vegan system and the Realm which specifies that freight in Vegan bottoms is dutiable only when consigned to ports in the Realm?"

"You speak Algolian, do you? You Heralds have not been underrated, but don't plan to lie your way out of this. Yes, I am aware of some such agreement as you mentioned. We shall board you, as I said, and assess and collect duty in kind. If, regrettably, there has been any mistake you are, of course, free to apply to the Realm for reimbursement. Now, heave to!"

"I have no intentions of lying. I speak the solemn truth when I say that we shall fight to the last man any attempt of yours to board and loot us."

Alen's mind was racing furiously through the catalogue of planetary folkways the Rule had decreed that he master. Algol IV—some ancestor-worship; veneration of mother; hand-to-hand combat with knives; complimentary greeting, "May you never strike down a weaker foe"; folk-hero Gaarek unjustly accused of slaying a cripple and exiled but it was an enemy's plot—

A disconcerted shadow was crossing the face of the officer as Alen improvised: "You will, of course, kill us all. But before this happens I shall have messaged back to the College and Order of Heralds the facts in the case, with a particular request that your family be informed. Your name, I think, will be remembered as long as Gaarek's—though not in the same way, of course; the Algolian whose hundred-man battle cruiser wiped out a virtually unarmed freighter with a crew of eight."

The officer's face was dark with rage. "You devil!" he snarled. "Leave my family out of this! I'll come aboard and fight you man-to-man if you have the stomach for it!"

Alen shook his head regretfully. "The Rule of my Order forbids recourse to violence," he said. "Our only permissible weapon is the truth."

"We're coming aboard," said the officer grimly. "I'll order my men not to harm your people. We'll just be collecting customs. If your people shoot first, my men will be under orders to do nothing more than disable them."

Alen smiled and uttered a sentence or two in Algolian.

The officer's jaw dropped and he croaked, after a pause: "I'll cut you to ribbons. You can't say that about my mother, you—" and he spewed back some of the words Alen had spoken.

"Calm yourself," said the Herald gravely. "I apologize for my disgusting and unheraldic remarks. But I wished to prove a point. You would have killed me if you could; I touched off a reaction which had been planted in you by your culture. I will be able to do the same with the men of yours who come aboard. For every race of man there is the intolerable insult that must be avenged in blood.

"Send your men aboard under orders not to kill if you wish; I shall goad them into a killing rage. We shall be massacred, yours will be the blame and you will be disgraced and disowned by your entire planet." Alen hoped desperately that the naval crews of the Realm were, as reputed, a barbarous and undisciplined lot—

Evidently they were, and the proud Algolian dared not risk it. In his native language he spat again: "You devil!" and switched back into Vegan. "Freighter *Starsong*," he said bleakly, "I find that my space fix was in error and that you are not in Realm territory. You may proceed."

The astrogator said from the detector board, incredulously: "He's disengaging. He's off us. He's accelerating. Herald *what* did you say to him?"

But the reaction from blackbeard was more gratifying.

Speechless, the trader took off his cap. Alen acknowledged the salute with a grave nod before he started back to his cubicle. It was just as well, he reflected, that the trader didn't know his life and his ship had been unconditionally pledged in a finish fight against a hundred-man battle cruiser.

Lyra's principal spaceport was pocked and broken, but they made a fair-enough landing. Alen, in full heraldic robes, descended from *Starsong* to greet a handful of port officials.

"Any metals aboard?" demanded one of them.

"None for sale," said the Herald.

"We have Vegan gems, chiefly triple-fire." He knew that the dull little planet was short of metals and, having made a virtue of necessity was somehow prejudiced against their import.

"Have your crew transfer the cargo to the Customs shed," said the port official studying *Starsong's* papers. "And all of you wait there."

All of them—except Alen—lugged numbered sacks and boxes of gems to the low brick building designated. The trader was allowed to pocket a handful for samples before the shed was sealed—a complicated business. A brick was mortared over the simple ironwood latch that closed the ironwood door, a pat of clay was slapped over the brick and the port seal stamped in it. A mechanic with what looked like a pottery blowtorch fed by powdered coal played a flame on the clay seal until it glowed orange-red and that was that.

"Herald," said the port official, "tell the merchant to sign here and make his fingerprints."

Alen studied the document; it was a simple identification form. Blackbeard signed with the reed pen provided and fingerprinted the documented. After two weeks in space he scarcely needed to ink his fingers first.

"Now tell him that we'll release the gems on his written fingerprinted order to whatever Lyran citizens he sells to. And explain that this roundabout system is necessary to avoid metal smuggling. Please remove *all* metal from your clothes and stow it on your ship. Then we will seal that, too, and put it under guard until you are ready to take off. We regret that we will have to search you before we turn you loose, but we can't afford to have our economy disrupted by irresponsible introduction of metals." Alen had not realized it was that bad.

After the thorough search that extended to the confiscation

of forgotten watches and pins, the port officials changed a sheaf of the trader's uranium-backed Vegan currency into Lyran legal tender based on man-hours. Blackbeard made a partial payment to the crew, told them to have a good liberty and check in at the port at sunset tomorrow for probable take-off.

Alen and the trader were driven to town in an unlikely vehicle whose power plant was a pottery turbine. The driver, when they were safely out on the open road, furtively asked whether they had any metal they wanted to discard.

The trader asked sharply in his broken Lyran: "What you do you get metal? Where sell, how use?"

The driver, following a universal tendency, raised his voice and lapsed into broken Lyran himself to tell the strangers: "Black market science men pay much, much for little bit metal. Study, use build. Politicians make law no metal, what I care politicians? But you no tell, gentlemen?"

"We won't tell," said Alen. "But we have no metal for you."

The driver shrugged.

"Herald," said the trader, "what do you make of it?"

"I didn't know it was a political issue. We concern ourselves with the basic patterns of a people's behavior, not the day-to-day expressions of the patterns. The planet's got no heavy metals, which means there were no metals available to the primitive Lyrans. The lighter metals don't occur in native form or in easily-split compounds. They proceeded along the ceramic line instead of the metallic line and appear to have done quite well for themselves up to a point. No electricity, of course, no aviation and no space flight."

"And," said the trader, "naturally the people who make these buggies and that blowtorch we saw are scared witless that metals will be imported and put them out of business. So naturally they have laws passed prohibiting it."

"Naturally," said the Herald, looking sharply at the trader. But blackbeard was back in character a moment later. "An outrage," he growled. "Trying to tell a man what he can and can't import when he sees a decent chance to make a bit of profit."

The driver dropped them at a boardinghouse. It was half-timbered construction, which appeared to be swankier than the more common brick. The floors were plate glass, roughened for traction. Alen got them a double room with a view.

"What's that thing?" demanded the trader, inspecting the view.

The thing was a structure looming above the slate and tile roofs of the town—a round brick tower for its first twenty-five meters and then wood for another fifteen. As they studied it, it pricked up a pair of ears at the top and began to flop them wildly.

"Semaphore," said Alen.

A minute later blackbeard piteously demanded from the bathroom: "*How* do you make water come out of the tap? I touched it all over but nothing happened."

"You have to turn it," said Alen, demonstrating. "And that thing—you pull it sharply down, hold it and then release."

"Barbarous," muttered the trader. "Barbarous."

An elderly maid came in to show them how to string their hammocks and ask if they happened to have a bit of metal to give her for a souvenir. They sent her away and, rather than face the public dining room, made a meal from their own stores and turned in for the night.

It's going well, thought Alen drowsily: going very well indeed.

He awoke abruptly, but made no move. It was dark in the double room, and there were stealthy, furtive little noises nearby. A hundred thoughts flashed through his head of Lyran treachery and double-dealing. He lifted his eyelids a trifle and saw a figure silhouetted against the faint light of the big window. If a burglar, he was a clumsy one.

There was a stirring from the other hammock, the trader's. With a subdued roar that sounded like "Thieving villains!" blackbeard launched himself from the hammock at the intruder. But his feet tangled in the hammock cords and he belly-flopped on the floor.

The burglar, if it was one, didn't dash smoothly and efficiently for the door. He straightened himself against the window and said resignedly: "You need not fear. I will make no resistance."

Alen rolled from the hammock and helped the trader to his feet. "He said he doesn't want to fight," he told the trader.

Blackbeard siezed the intruder and shook him like a rat.

"So the rogue is a coward too!" he boomed. "Give us a light, Herald."

Alen uncovered the slow-match, blew it to a flame, squeakily pumped up a pressure torch until a jet of pulverized coal sprayed from its nozzle and ignited it. A dozen strokes more and there was enough heat feeding back from the jet to maintain the pressure cycle.

Through all of this the trader was demanding in his broken Lyran: "What make here, thief? What reason thief us room?"

The Herald brought the hissing pressure lamp to the window. The intruder's face was not the unhealthy, neurotic face of a criminal. Its thin lines told of discipline and thought.

"What did you want here?" asked Alen.

"Metal," said the intruder simply. "I thought you might have a bit of iron."

It was the first time a specific metal had been named by any Lyran. He used, of course, the Vegan word for iron.

"You are particular," remarked the Herald. "Why iron?"

"I have heard that it possesses certain properties—perhaps you can tell me before you turn me over to the police. Is it true, as we hear, that a mass of iron whose crystals have been aligned by a sharp blow will strongly attract another piece of iron with a force related to the distance between them?"

"It is true," said the Herald, studying the man's face. It was lit with excitement. Deliberately Alen added: "This alignment is more easily and uniformly effected by placing the mass of iron in an electric field—that is, a space surrounding the passage of an electron stream through a conductor." Many of the words he used had to be Vegan; there were no Lyran words for "electric," "electron" or "conductor."

The intruder's face fell. "I have tried to master the concept you refer to," he admitted. "But it is beyond me. I have questioned other interstar voyagers and they have touched on it, but I cannot grasp it— But thank you, sir; you have been very courteous. I will trouble you no further while you summon the watch."

"You give up too easily," said Alen. "For a scientist, much too easily. If we turn you over to the watch, there will be hearings and testimony and whatnot. Our time is limited here on your planet; I doubt that we can spare any for your legal processes."

The trader let go of the intruder's shoulder and grumbled:

"Why you no ask we have iron, I tell you no. Search, search, take all metal away. We no police you. I sorry hurted you arms. Here for you." Blackbeard brought out a palmful of his sample gems and picked out a large triple-fire stone. "You not be angry me," he said, putting it in the Lyran's hand.

"I can't—" said the scientist.

Blackbeard closed his fingers over the stone and growled: "I give, you take. Maybe buy iron with, eh?"

"That's so," said the Lyran. "Thank you both, gentlemen. Thank you—"

"You go," said the trader. "You go, we sleep again."

The scientist bowed with dignity and left their room.

"Gods of space," swore the trader. "To think that Jukkl, the *Starsong's* wiper, knows more about electricity and magnetism than a brainy fellow like that."

"And they are the key to physics," mused Alen. "A scientist here is dead-ended forever, because their materials are all insulators! Glass, clay, glaze, wood."

"Funny, all right," yawned blackbeard. "Did you see me collar him once I got on my feet? Sharp, eh? Good night, Herald." He gruntingly hauled himself into the hammock again, leaving Alen to turn off the hissing light and cover the slow-match with its perforated lid.

They had roast fowl of some sort or other for breakfast in the public dining room. Alen was required by his Rule to refuse the red wine that went with it. The trader gulped it approvingly. "A sensible, though backward people," he said. "And now if you'll inquire of the management where the thievish jewel-buyers congregate, we can get on with our business and perhaps be off by dawn tomorrow."

"So quickly?" asked Alen, almost forgetting himself enough to show surprise.

"My charter on *Starsong*, good Herald—thirty days to go, but what might not go wrong in space? And then there would be penalties to mulct me of whatever minute profit I may realize."

Alen learned that Gromeg's Tavern was the gem mart and they took another of the turbine-engined cabs through the brick-paved streets.

Gromeg's was a dismal, small-windowed brick barn with heavy-set men lounging about, an open kitchen at one end and tables at the other. A score of smaller, sharp-faced men were at the tables sipping wine and chatting.

"I am Journeyman-Herald Alen," announced Alen clearly, "with Vegan gems to dispose of."

There was a silence of elaborate unconcern, and then one of the dealers spat and grunted: "Vegan gems. A drug on the market. Take them away, Herald."

"Come, master trader," said Alen in the Lyran tongue. "The gem dealers of Lyra do not want your wares." He started for the door.

One of the dealers called languidly: "Well, wait a moment. I have nothing better to do; since you've come all this way I'll have a look at your stuff."

"You honor us," said Alen. He and blackbeard sat at the man's table. The trader took out a palmful of samples, counted them meaningfully and laid them on the boards.

"Well," said the gem dealer, "I don't know whether to be amused or insulted. I am Garthkint, the gem dealer—not a retailer of *beads*. However, I have no hard feelings. A drink for your frowning friend, Herald? I know you gentry don't indulge." The drink was already on the table, brought by one of the hulking guards.

Alen passed Garthkint's own mug of wine to the trader, explaining politely: "In my master trader's native Cepheus it is considered honorable for the guest to sip the drink his host laid down and none other. A charming custom, is it not?"

"Charming, though unsanitary," muttered the gem dealer—and he did not touch the drink he had ordered for blackbeard.

"I can't understand a word either of you is saying—too flowery. Was this little rat trying to drug me?" demanded the trader in Cephean.

"No," said Alen. "Just trying to get you drunk." To Garthkint in Lyran, he explained, "The good trader was saying that he wishes to leave at once. I was agreeing with him."

"Well," said Garthkint, "perhaps I can take a couple of your gauds. For some youngster who wishes a cheap ring."

"He's getting to it," Alen told the trader.

"High time," grunted blackbeard.

"The trader asks me to inform you," said Alen, switching back to Lyran, "that he is unable to sell in lots smaller than five hundred gems."

"A compact language, Cephean," said Garthkint, narrowing his eyes.

"Is it not?" Alen blandly agreed.

The gem dealer's forefinger rolled an especially fine three-fire stone from the little pool of gems on the table. "I suppose," he said grudgingly, "that this is what I must call the best of the lot. What, I am curious to know, is the price you would set for five hundred equal in quality and size to this poor thing?"

"This," said Alen, "is the good trader's first venture to your delightful planet. He wishes to be remembered and welcomed all of the many times he anticipates returning. Because of this he has set an absurdly low price, counting good will as more important than a prosperous voyage. Two thousand Lyran credits."

"Absurd," snorted Garthkint. "I cannot do business with you. Either you are insanely rapacious or you have been pitifully misguided as to the value of your wares. I am well-known for my charity; I will assume that the latter is the case. I trust you will not be too downcast when I tell you that five hundred of these muddy, undersized out-of-round objects are worth no more than two hundred credits."

"If you are serious," said Alen with marked amazement, "we would not dream of imposing on you. At the figure you mention, we might as well not sell at all but return with our wares to Cepheus and give these gems to children in the streets for marbles. Good gem trader, excuse us for taking up so much of your time and many thanks for your warm hospitality in the matter of the wine." He switched to Cephean and said: "We're dickering now. Two thousand and two hundred. Get up; we're going to start to walk out."

"What if he lets us go?" grumbled blackbeard, but he did heave himself to his feet and turn to the door as Alen rose.

"My trader echoes my regrets," the Herald said in Lyran. "Farewell."

"Well, stay a moment," said Garthkint. "I am well-known for my soft heart toward strangers. A charitable man might go as high as five hundred and absorb the inevitable loss. If you should return some day with a passable lot of *real* gems, it would be worth my while for you to remember who treated you with such benevolence and give me fair choice."

"Noble Lyran," said Alen, apparently almost overcome. "I

shall not easily forget your combination of acumen and charity. It is a lesson to traders. It is a lesson to me. I shall *not* insist on two thousand. I shall cut the throat of my trader's venture by reducing his price to eighteen hundred credits, though I wonder how I shall dare tell him of it."

"What's going on now?" demanded blackbeard.

"Five hundred and eighteen hundred," said Alen. "We can sit down again."

"Up, down—up, down," muttered the trader.

They sat, and Alen said in Lyran: "My trader unexpectedly indorses the reduction. He says, 'Better to lose some than all' —an old proverb in the Cephean tongue. And he forbids any further reduction."

"Come, now," wheedled the gem dealer. "Let us be men of the world about this. One must give a little and take a little. Everybody knows he can't have his own way forever. I shall offer a good, round eight hundred credits and we'll close on it, eh? Pilquis, fetch us a pen and ink!" One of the burly guards was right there with an inkpot and a reed pen. Garthkint had a Customs form out of his tunic and was busily filling it in to specify the size, number and fire of gems to be released to him.

"What's it now?" asked blackbeard.

"Eight hundred."

"Take it!"

"Garthkint," said Alen regretfully, "you heard the firmness and decision in my trader's voice? What can I do? I am only speaking for him. He is a hard man but perhaps I can talk him around later. I offer you the gems at a ruinous fifteen hundred credits."

"Split the difference," said Garthkint resignedly.

"Done at eleven-fifty," said Alen.

That blackbeard understood. "Well done!" he boomed at Alen and took a swig at Garthkint's winecup. "Have him fill in 'Sack eighteen' on his paper. It's five hundred of that grade."

The gem dealer counted out twenty-three fifty-credit notes and blackbeard signed and fingerprinted the release.

"Now," said Garthkint, "you will please remain here while I take a trip to the spaceport for my property." Three or four of the guards were suddenly quite close.

"You will find," said Alen dryly, "that our standard of commercial morality is no lower than yours."

The dealer smiled politely and left.

"Who will be the next?" asked Alen of the room at large.

"I'll look at your gems," said another dealer, sitting at the table.

With the ice-breaking done, the transactions went quicker. Alen had disposed of a dozen lots by the time their first buyer returned.

"It's all right," he said. "We've been tricked before, but your gems are as represented. I congratulate you, Herald, on driving a hard, fair bargain."

"That means," said Alen regretfully, "that I should have asked for more." The guards were once more lounging in corners and no longer seemed so menacing.

They had a mid-day meal and continued to dispose of their wares. At sunset Alen held a final auction to clean up the odd lots that remained over and was urged to stay to dinner.

The trader, counting a huge wad of the Lyran manpower-based notes, shook his head. "We should be off before dawn, Herald," he told Alen. "Time is money, time is money."

"They are very insistent."

"And I am very stubborn. Thank them and let us be on our way before anything else is done to increase my overhead."

Something did turn up—a city watchman with a bloody nose and split lip.

He demanded of the Herald: "Are you responsible for the Cephean maniac known as Elwon?"

Garthkint glided up to mutter in Alen's ear: "Beware how you answer!"

Alen needed no warning. His grounding included Lyran legal concepts—and on the backward little planet touched with many relics of feudalism "responsible" covered much territory.

"What has Chief Elwon done?" he parried.

"As you see," the watchman glumly replied, pointing to his wounds. "And the same to three others before we got him out of the wrecked wineshop and into the castle. Are you responsible for him?"

"Let me speak with my trader for a moment. Will you have some wine meantime?" He signaled and one of the guards brought a mug.

"Don't mind if I do. I can use it," sighed the watchman.

"We are in trouble," said Alen to blackbeard. "Chief Elwon is in the 'castle'—prison—for drunk and disorderly conduct. You as his master are considered responsible for his conduct under Lyran law. You must pay his fines or serve his penalties. Or you can 'disown' him, which is considered dishonorable but sometimes necessary. For paying his fine or serving his time you have a prior lien on his services, without pay—but of course that's unenforceable off Lyra."

Blackbeard was sweating a little. "Find out from the policeman how long all this is likely to take. I don't want to leave Elwon here and I do want us to get off as soon as possible. Keep him occupied, now, while I go about some business."

The trader retreated to a corner of the darkening barnlike tavern, beckoning Garthkint and a guard with him as Alen returned to the watchman.

"Good keeper of the peace," he said, "will you have another?"

He would.

"My trader wishes to know what penalties are likely to be levied against the unfortunate Chief Elwon."

"Going to leave him in the lurch, eh?" asked the watchman a little belligerently. "A fine master you have!"

One of the dealers at the table indignantly corroborated him. "If you foreigners aren't prepared to live up to your obligations, why did you come here in the first place? What happens to business if a master can send his man to steal and cheat and then say: 'Don't blame *me*—it was *his* doing!'"

Alen patiently explained: "On other planets, good Lyrans, the tie of master and man is not so strong that a man would obey if he were ordered to go and steal or cheat."

They shook their heads and muttered. It was unheard-of.

"Good watchman," pressed the Herald, "my trader does not *want* to disown Chief Elwon. Can you tell me what recompense would be necessary—and how long it would take to manage the business?"

The watchman started on a third cup which Alen had unostentatiously signaled for. "It's hard to say," he told the Herald weightily. "For my damages, I would demand a hundred credits at least. The three other members of the watch battered by your lunatic could ask no less. The wineshop suffered easily five hundred credits' damage. The owner of it was beaten, but that doesn't matter, of course."

"No imprisonment?"

"Oh, a flogging, of course"—Alen started before he recalled that the "flogging" was a few half-hearted symbolic strokes on the covered shoulders with a light cane—"but no imprisonment. His Honor, Judge Krarl, does not sit on the night bench. Judge Krarl is a newfangled reformer, stranger. He professes to believe that mulcting is unjust—that it makes it easy for the rich to commit crime and go scot-free."

"But doesn't it?" asked Alen, drawn off-course in spite of himself. There was pitying laughter around him.

"Look you," a dealer explained kindly. "The good watchman suffers battery, the mad Cephean or his master is mulcted for damages, the watchman is repaid for his injuries. What kind of justice is it to the watchman if the mad Cephean is locked away in a cell unfined?"

The watchman nodded approvingly. "Well-said," he told the dealer. "Luckily we have on the night bench a justice of the old school, His Honor, Judge Treel. Stern, but fair. You should hear him! 'Fifty credits! A hundred credits and the lash! Robbed a ship, eh? Two thousand credits!'" He returned to his own voice and said with awe: "For a murder, he never assesses less than *ten thousand credits!*"

And if the murderer couldn't pay, Alen knew, he became a "public charge," "responsible to the state"—that is, a slave. If he could pay, of course, he was turned loose.

"And His Honor, Judge Treel," he pressed, "is sitting to-night? Can we possibly appear before him, pay the fines and be off?"

"To be sure, stranger. I'd be a fool if I waited until morning, wouldn't I?" The wine had loosened his tongue a little too far and he evidently realized it. "Enough of this," he said. "Does your master honorably accept responsibility for the Cephean? If so, come along with me, the two of you, and we'll get this over with."

"Thanks, good watchman. We are coming."

He went to blackbeard, now alone in his corner, and said: "It's all right. We can pay off—about a thousand credits— and be on our way."

The trader muttered darkly: "Lyran jurisdiction or not, it's coming out of Elwon's pay. The bloody fool!"

They rattled through the darkening streets of the town in

one of the turbine-powered wagons, the watchman sitting up front with the driver and the trader and the Herald behind.

"Something's burning," said Alen to the trader, sniffing the air.

"This stinking buggy—" began blackbeard. "Oops," he said, interrupting himself and slapping at his cloak.

"Let me, trader," said Alen. He turned back the cloak, licked his thumb, and rubbed out a crawling ring of sparks spreading across a few centimeters of the cloak's silk lining. And he looked fixedly at what had started the little fire. It was an improperly-covered slow-match protruding from a holstered device that was unquestionably a hand weapon.

"I bought it from one of their guards while you were parleying with the policeman," explained blackbeard embarrassedly. "I had a time making him understand. That Garthkint fellow helped." He fiddled with the perforated cover of the slow-match, screwing it on more firmly.

"A pitiful excuse for a weapon," he went on, carefully arranging his cloak over it. "The trigger isn't a trigger and the thumb-safety isn't a safety. You pump the trigger a few times to build up pressure, and a little air squirts out to blow the match to life. Then you uncover the match and pull back the cocking-piece. This levers a dart into the barrel. *Then* you push the thumb-safety which puffs coaldust into the firing chamber and also swivels down the slow-match onto a touchhole. *Poof*, and away goes the dart if you didn't forget any of the steps or do them in the wrong order. Luckily, I also got a knife."

He patted the nape of his neck and said, "That's where they carry 'em here. A little sheath between the shoulderblades—wonderful for a fast draw-and-throw, though it exposes you a little more than I like when you reach. The knife's black glass. Splendid edge and good balance.

"And the thieving Lyrans knew they had me where it hurt. Seven thousand, five hundred credits for the knife and gun— if you can call it that—and the holsters. By rights I should dock Elwon for them, the bloody fool. Still, it's better to buy his way out and leave no hard feelings behind us, eh, Herald?"

"Incomparably better," said Alen. "And I am amazed that you even entertained the idea of an armed jail-delivery. What if Chief Elwon had to serve a few days in a prison? Would that be worse than forever barring yourself from the planet and blackening the names of all traders with Lyra? Trader, do not hope to put down the credits that your weapons cost you as a legitimate expense of the voyage. I will not allow it when I audit your books. It was a piece of folly on which you spent personal funds, as far as the College and Order of Heralds is concerned."

"Look here," protested blackbeard. "You're supposed to be spreading utilitarian civilization, aren't you? What's utilitarian about leaving one of my crewmen here?"

Alen ignored the childish argument and wrapped himself in angry silence. As to civilization, he wondered darkly whether such a trading voyage and his part in it was relevant at all. Were the slanders true? Was the College and Order simply a collection of dupes headed by cynical oldsters greedy for luxury and power?

Such thoughts hadn't crossed his mind in a long time. He'd been too busy to entertain them, cramming his head with languages, folk-ways, mores, customs, underlying patterns of culture, of hundreds of galactic peoples—and for what? So that this fellow could make a profit and the College and Order take a quarter of that profit. If civilization was to come to Lyra, it would have to come in the form of metal. If the Lyrans didn't want metal, *make* them take it.

What did Machiavelli say? "The chief foundations of all states are good laws and good arms; and as there cannot be good laws where the state is not well-armed, it follows that where they are well-armed, they have good laws." It was odd that the teachers had slurred over such a seminal idea, emphasizing instead the spiritual integrity of the weaponless College and Order—or was it?

The disenchantment he felt creeping over him was terrifying.

"The castle," said the watchman over his shoulder, and their wagon stopped with a rattle before a large but unimpressive brick structure of five stories.

"You wait," the trader told the driver after they got out. He handed him two of his fifty-credit bills. "You wait, you get many, many more money. You understand, wait?"

"I wait plenty much," shouted the driver delightedly. "I wait all night, all day. You wonderful master. You great, great master, I wait—"

"All right," growled the trader, shutting him off. "You wait."

The watchman took them through an entrance hall lit by hissing pressure lamps and casually guarded by a few liveried men with truncheons. He threw open the door of a medium-sized, well-lit room with a score of people in it, looked in, and uttered a despairing groan.

A personage on a chair that looked like a throne said sharply, "Are those the star-travelers? Well, don't just stand there. Bring them in!"

"Yes, your honor, Judge Krarl," said the watchman unhappily.

"It's the wrong judge!" Alen hissed at the trader. "This one gives out jail sentences!"

"Do what you can," said blackbeard grimly.

The watchman guided them to the personage in the chair and indicated a couple of low stools, bowed to the chair and retired to stand at the back of the room.

"Your honor," said Alen, "I am Journeyman-Herald Alen, Herald for the trading voyage—"

"Speak when you're spoken to," said the judge sharply. "Sir, with the usual insolence of wealth you have chosen to keep us waiting. I do not take this personally; it might have happened to Judge Treel, who—to your evident dismay—I am replacing because of a sudden illness, or to any other member of the bench. But as an insult to our justice, we cannot overlook it. Sir, consider yourself reprimanded. Take your seats. Watchman, bring in the Cephean."

"Sit down," Alen murmured to the trader. "This is going to be bad."

A watchman brought in Chief Elwon, bleary-eyed, tousled and sporting a few bruises. He gave Alen and the trader a shamefaced grin as his guard sat him on a stool beside them. The trader glared back.

Judge Krarl mumbled perfunctorily: "Letbattlebejoined amongtheseveralpartiesinthisdisputeletnomanquestionourimpartialawardingofthevictoryspeaknowifyouyieldinsteadtoour judgment. *Well?* Speak up, you watchmen!"

The watchman who had brought the Herald and the trader started and said from the back of the room: "Iyieldinsteadto yourhonorsjudgment."

Three other watchmen and a battered citizen, the wineshop

keeper, mumbled in turn: "Iyieldinsteadtoyourhonorsjudgment."

"Herald, speak for the accused," snapped the judge.

Well, thought Alen, I can try. "Your Honor," he said,
"Chief Elwon's master does not yield to your honor's judgment. He is ready to battle the other parties in the dispute
or their masters."

"What insolence is this?" screamed the judge, leaping from
his throne. "The barbarous customs of other worlds do not
prevail in this court! Who spoke of battle—?" He shut his
mouth with a snap, evidently abruptly realizing that *he* had
spoken of battle, in an archaic phrase that harked back to
the origins of justice on the planet. The judge sat down again
and told Alen, more calmly: "You have mistaken a mere
formality. The offer was not made in earnest." Obviously, he
didn't like the sound of that himself, but he proceeded, "Now
say 'Iyieldinsteadtoyourhonorsjudgment', and we can get on
with it. For your information, trial by combat has not been
practiced for many generations on our enlightened planet."

Alen said politely: "Your Honor, I am a stranger to many
of the ways of Lyra, but our excellent College and Order of
Heralds instructed me well in the underlying principles of
your law. I recall that one of your most revered legal maxims
declares: 'The highest crime against man is murder; the highest crime against man's society is breach of promise.'"

Purpling, the judge snarled: "Are you presuming to bandy
law with me, you slippery-tongued foreigner? Are you presuming to accuse me of the high crime of breaking my promise?
For your information, a promise consists of an offer to do,
or refrain from doing, a thing in return for a consideration.
There must be the five elements of promiser, promisee, offer,
substance, and consideration."

"If you will forgive a foreigner," said Alen, suddenly feeling
the ground again under his feet, "I maintain that you offered
the parties in the dispute your services in awarding the
victory."

"An empty argument," snorted the judge. "Just as an offer
with substance from somebody to nobody for a consideration
is no promise, or an offer without substance from somebody
to somebody for a consideration is no promise, so my offer
was no promise, for there was no consideration involved."

"Your honor, must the consideration be from the promisee to the promiser?"

"Of course not. A third party may provide the consideration."

"Then I respectfully maintain that your offer was a promise, since a third party, the government, provided you with the considerations of salary and position in return for you offering your services to the disputants."

"Watchmen, clear the room of disinterested persons," said the judge hoarsely. While it was being done, Alen swiftly filled in the trader and Chief Elwon. Blackbeard grinned at the mention of a five-against-one battle royal, and the engineer looked alarmed.

When the doors closed leaving the nine of them in privacy, the judge said bitterly: "Herald, where did you learn such devilish tricks?"

Alen told him: "My College and Order instructed me well. A similar situation existed on a planet called England during an age known as the Victorious. Trial by combat had long been obsolete, there as here, but had never been declared so —there as here. A litigant won a hopeless lawsuit by publishing a challenge to his opponent and appearing at the appointed place in full armor. His opponent ignored the challenge and so lost the suit by default. The English dictator, one Disraeli, hastily summoned his parliament to abolish trial by combat."

"And so," mused the judge, "I find myself accused in my own chamber of high crime if I do not permit you five to slash away at each other and decide who won."

The wineshop keeper began to blubber that he was a peaceable man and didn't intend to be carved up by that blackbearded, bloodthirsty star-traveler. All he wanted was his money.

"Silence!" snapped the judge. "Of course there will be no combat. Will you, shopkeeper, and you watchmen, withdraw if you receive satisfactory financial settlements?"

They would.

"Herald, you may dicker with them."

The four watchmen stood fast by their demand for a hundred credits apiece, and got it. The terrified shopkeeper regained his balance and demanded a thousand. Alen explained that his black-bearded master from a rude and impetuous world might be unable to restrain his rage when he, Alen, interpreted the demand and, ignoring the consequences, might beat him, the shopkeeper, to a pulp. The asking price plunged to a reasonable five hundred, which was paid over. The shopkeeper got the judge's permission to leave and backed out, bowing.

"You see, trader," Alen told blackbeard, "that it was needless to buy weapons when the spoken word—"

"And now," said the judge with a sneer, "we are easily out of *that* dilemma. Watchmen, arrest the three star-travelers and take them to the cages."

"Your honor!" cried Alen, outraged.

"Money won't get you out of *this* one. I charge you with treason."

"The charge is obsolete—" began the Herald hotly, but he broke off as he realized the vindictive strategy.

"Yes, it is. And one of its obsolete provisions is that treason charges must be tried by the parliament at a regular session, which isn't due for two hundred days. You'll be freed and I may be reprimanded, but by my head, for two hundred days you'll regret that you made a fool of *me*. Take them away."

"A trumped-up charge against us. Prison for two hundred days," said Alen swiftly to the trader as the watchmen closed in.

"Why buy weapons?" mocked the blackbeard, showing his teeth. His left arm whipped up and down, there was a black streak through the air—and the judge was pinned to his throne with a black glass knife through his throat and the sneer of triumph still on his lips.

The trader, before the knife struck, had the clumsy pistol out, with the cover off the glowing match and the cocking piece back. He must have pumped and cocked it under his cloak, thought Alen numbly as he told the watchmen, without prompting: "Get back against the wall and turn around." They did. They wanted to live, and the grinning blackbeard who had made meat of the judge with a flick of the arm was a terrifying figure.

"Well done, Alen," said the trader. "Take their clubs, El-won. Two for you, two for the Herald. Alen, don't argue! I had to kill the judge before he raised an alarm—nothing but death will silence his breed. You may have to kill too before we're out of this. Take the clubs." He passed the clumsy pistol to Chief Elwon and said: "Keep it on their backs. The thing that looks like a thumb-safety is a trigger. Put a dart through the first one who tries to make a break. Alen, tell the fellow on the end to turn around and come to me slowly."

Alen did. Blackbeard swiftly stripped him, tore and knotted his clothes into ropes and bound and gagged him. The others got the same treatment in less than ten minutes.

The trader holstered the gun and rolled the watchmen out of the line of sight from the door of the chamber. He recovered his knife and wiped it on the judge's shirt. Alen had to help him prop the body behind the throne's high back.

"Hide those clubs," blackbeard said. "Straight faces. Here we go."

They went out, single file, opening the door only enough to pass. Alen, last in line, told one of the liveried guards nearby: "His honor, Judge Krarl, does not wish to be disturbed."

"That's news?" asked the tipstaff sardonically. He put his hand on the Herald's arm. "Only yesterday he gimme a blast when I brought him a mug of water he asked me for himself. An outrageous interruption, he called me, and he asked for the water himself. What do you think of that?"

"Terrible," said Alen hastily. He broke away and caught up with the trader and the engineer at the entrance hall. Idlers and loungers were staring at them as they headed for the waiting wagon.

"I wait!" the driver told them loudly. "I wait long, much. You pay more, more?"

"We pay more," said the trader. "You start."

The driver brought out a smoldering piece of punk, lit a pressure torch, lifted the barn-door section of the wagon's floor to expose the pottery turbine and preheated it with the torch. He pumped squeakily for minutes, spinning a flywheel with his other hand, before the rotor began to turn on its own. Down went the hatch, up onto the seats went the passengers.

"The spaceport," said Alen. With a slate-pencil screech the driver engaged his planetary gear and they were off.

Through it all, blackbeard had ignored frantic muttered questions from Chief Elwon, who had wanted nothing to do with murder, especially of a judge. "You sit up there," growled the trader, "and every so often you look around and see if we're being followed. Don't alarm the driver. And if we get to the spaceport and blast off without any trouble, keep your story to yourself." He settled down in the back seat with Alen and maintained a gloomy silence. The young Herald was too much in awe of this stranger, so suddenly competent in assorted forms of violence, to question him.

They did get to the spaceport without trouble, and found the crew in the Customs shed, emptied of the gems by dealers with releases. They had built a fire for warmth.

"We wish to leave immediately," said the trader, to the port officer. "Can you change my Lyran currency?"

The officers began to sputter apologetically that it was late and the vault was sealed for the night—

"That's all right. We'll change it on Vega. It'll get back to you. Call off your guards and unseal our ship."

They followed the port officer to *Starsong's* dim bulk out on the field. The officer cracked the seal on her with his club in the light of a flaring pressure lamp held by one of the guards.

Alen was sweating hard through it all. As they started across the field he had seen what looked like two closely spaced green stars low on the horizon towards town suddenly each jerk up and towards each other in minute arcs. The semaphore!

The signal officer in the port administration building would be watching too—but nobody on the field, preoccupied with the routine of departure, seemed to have noticed.

The lights flipped this way and that. Alen didn't know the code and bitterly regretted the lack. After some twenty signals the lights flipped to the "rest" postion again as the port officer was droning out a set of take-off regulations: bearing, height above settled areas, permissible atomic fuels while in atmosphere—Alen saw somebody start across the field toward them from the administration building. The guards were leaning on their long, competent looking weapons.

Alen inconspicuously detached himself from the group around *Starsong* and headed across the dark field to meet the approaching figure. Nearing it, he called out a low greeting in Lyran, using the noncom-to-officer military form.

"Sergeant," said the signal officer quietly, "go and draw off the men a few meters from the star-travelers. Tell them the ship mustn't leave, that they're to cover the foreigners and shoot if—"

Alen stood dazedly over the limp body of the signal officer. And then he quickly hid the bludgeon again and strolled back to the ship, wondering whether he'd cracked the Lyran's skull.

The port was open by then and the crew filing in. He was last. "Close it fast," he told the trader. "I had to—"

"I saw you," grunted blackbeard. "A semaphore message?" He was working as he spoke, and the metal port closed.

"Astrogator and engineer, take over," he told them.

"All hands to their bunks," ordered Astrogator Hufner. "Blast-off immediate."

Alen took to his cubicle and strapped himself in. Blast-off deafened him, rattled his bones and made him thoroughly sick as usual. After what seemed like several wretched hours, they were definitely space-borne under smooth acceleration, and his nausea subsided.

Blackbeard knocked, came in, and unbuckled him.

"Ready to audit the books of the voyage?" asked the trader.

"No," said Alen feebly.

"It can wait," said the trader. "The books are the least important part, anyway. We have headed off a frightful war."

"War? We have?"

"War between Eyolf's Realm and Vega. It is the common gossip of chancelleries and trade missions that both governments have cast longing eyes on Lyrane, that they have plans to penetrate its economy by supplying metals to the planet without metals—by force, if need be. Alen, we have removed the pretext by which Eyolf's Realm and Vega would have attempted to snap up Lyrane and inevitably have come into conflict. Lyra is getting its metal now, and without imperialist entanglements."

"I saw none," the Herald said blankly.

"You wondered why I was in such haste to get off Lyra, and why I wouldn't leave Elwon there. It is because our Vegan gems were most unusual gems. I am not a technical man, but I understand they are actual gems which were treated to produce a certain effect at just about this time."

Blackbeard glanced at his wrist chronometer and said dreamily: "Lyra is getting metal. Wherever there is one of our gems, pottery is decomposing into its constituent aluminum, silicon, and oxygen. Fluxes and glazes are decomposing into calcium, zinc, barium, potassium, chromium, *and iron*. Buildings are crumbling, pants are dropping as ceramic belt-buckles disintegrate—"

"It means chaos!" protested Alen.

"It means civilization and peace. An ugly clash was in the making." Blackbeard paused and added deliberately: "Where neither their property nor their honor is touched, most men live content."

" 'The Prince', Chapter 19. You are—"

"There was another important purpose to the voyage," said the trader, grinning. "You will be interested in this." He handed Alen a document which, unfolded, had the seal of the College and Order at its head.

Alen read in a daze: "Examiner 19 to the Rector—final clearance of Novice—"

He lingered pridefully over the paragraph that described how he had "with coolness and great resource" foxed the battle cruiser of the Realm, "adapting himself readily in a delicate situation requiring not only physical courage but swift recall, evaluation and application of a minor planetary culture."

Not so pridefully he read: "—inclined towards pomposity of manner somewhat ludicrous in one of his years, though not unsuccessful in dominating the crew by his bearing—"

And: "—highly profitable disposal of our gems; a feat of no mean importance since the College and Order must, after all, maintain itself."

And: "—cleared the final and crucial hurdle with some mental turmoil if I am any judge, but did clear it. After some twenty years of indoctrination in unrealistic non-violence, the youth was confronted with a situation where nothing but violence would serve, correctly evaluated this, and applied violence in the form of a truncheon to the head of a Lyran signal officer, thereby demonstrating an ability to learn and common sense as precious as it is rare."

And, finally, simply: "Recommended for training."

"Training?" gasped Alen. "You mean there's more?"

"Not for most, boy. Not for most. The bulk of us are what we seem to be: oily, gun-shy, indispensable adjuncts to trade who feather our nest with percentages. We need those percentages and we need gun-shy Heralds."

Alen recited slowly: "Among other evils which being unarmed brings you, it causes you to be despised."

"Chapter 14," said blackbeard mechanically. "We leave such clues lying by their bedsides for twenty years, and they never notice them. For the few of us who do—more training."

"Will I learn to throw a knife like you?" asked Alen, repelled and fascinated at once by the idea.

"On your own time, if you wish. Mostly it's ethics and morals so you'll be able to weigh the values of such things as knife-throwing."

"Ethics! Morals!"

"We started as missionaries, you know."

"Everybody knows that. But the Great Utilitarian Reform —"

"Some of us," said blackbeard dryly, "think it was neither great, nor utilitarian, nor a reform."

It was a staggering idea. "But we're spreading utilitarian civilization!" protested Alen. "Or if we're not, what's the sense of it all?"

Blackbeard told him: "We have our different motives. One is a sincere utilitarian; another is a gambler—happy when he's in danger and his pulses are pounding. Another is proud and likes to trick people. More than a few conceive themselves as servants of mankind. I'll let you rest for a bit now." He rose.

"But you?" asked Alen hesitantly.

"Me? You will find me in Chapter Twenty-Six," grinned blackbeard. "And perhaps you'll find someone else." He closed the door behind him.

Alen ran through the chapter in his mind, puzzled, until—that was it.

It had a strange and inevitable familiarity to it as if he had always known that he would be saying it aloud, welcomingly, in this cramped cubicle aboard a battered starship:

"God is not willing to do everything, and thus take away our free will and that share of glory which belongs to us."

ABOUT C. M. KORNBLUTH

WHEN, after a long and impressive career in the science-fiction magazines, C. M. Kornbluth published his first novel, TAKEOFF, the *New York Herald Tribune* predicted that the book "should establish him firmly among the top-flight contemporaries in the field." That was all of two years ago. Since then there have appeared THE SPACE MERCHANTS, written with Frederik Pohl; THE SYNDIC; SEARCH THE SKY (with Pohl again); a pseudonymous historical novel; and a number of science-fiction short stories and novelettes—the latest of which, "Gomez," makes its first appearance in print in this collection.

Since his first published story appeared fourteen years ago, it is hard to realize that Mr. Kornbluth is still just a shade past thirty. "I was born in New York City in 1923," he writes, "and was educated in the city schools as far as freshman year at C. C. N. Y. when I was dropped for the usual reasons. I had already begun to contribute to the science-fiction magazines and became a full-time writer after leaving college, though most people regarded me as an unemployed bum. I weakened once to the extent of getting a job as a hand-screw-machine operator, but quit after a few months to enlist in the army. In three years of service I acquired a wife, a combat infantry badge, two ETO campaign stars, a PFC stripe, and a constant ringing in the ears. After my discharge I settled in Chicago where I combined writing blood-and-guts detective stories with acquiring an education according to the precepts of the University of Chicago. A friend managing the local bureau of a moribund news agency got me a job on its desk, and it was good-by, Chancellor Hutchins. I rose to bureau chief eventually, paralleling the news job with contributions to the science-fiction magazines and such fantastic chores as writing a syndicated review of phonograph records for children. In 1951, at the urging of my wife, my agent, and my doctor, I resigned my job to come east as a full-time free-lance writer again. Since then I've sired two children and eleven books, including this one. I live now in a Tioga County, New York, farm house, and visit New York City infrequently. I drive a senile Ford timidly and not well; I like to cook, specializing in Italian and Chinese dishes. I have been accused of being a compulsive reader. My writing habits have changed over the years from white-hot all-night sessions to a-little-every-day and plenty of polishing. I have no formal hobbies, but am interested in practically every human activity except sports. I have no settled opinions about writing; currently I'm concerned most over the invasion of science fiction by exponents of the so-called 'mandarin style.' "

BALLANTINE SCIENCE FICTION
3 Classics For $1.50 Post Free

F562 CAVIAR by Theodore Sturgeon

"Sturgeon is a prime example of the maturation of S-F over the past couple of decades . . . this volume points up his mastery of plot, technique and suspense." *Galaxy*

**F570 GLADIATOR-AT-LAW by Frederik Pohl &
C. M. Kornbluth**

When first published in 1955 this novel was greeted with enthusiasm all over the country. This is top-drawer science fiction and top-drawer writing.

F580 THE OCTOBER COUNTRY by Ray Bradbury

This book presents nineteen stories—the best from the long out of print limited edition of DARK CARNIVAL, plus five new and equally brilliant selections. The stories are awesome, macabre and a must for S-F readers.

A SCIENCE FICTION CLASSIC
NOW AVAILABLE FOR THE FIRST TIME
IN A PAPERBOUND EDITION

H. G. Wells, honored today as the pioneer writer in science fiction, is still unsurpassed in the power of his imagination and in his ability to forecast the future.

The First Men in the Moon is one of Wells's most fascinating novels—a book as strange as any you have ever read, and packed with unforgettable scenes, from the first flesh-crawling view of the monstrous life forms of the Moon, to the fight in the cave of the Selenites and the last, haunting message from the lone survivor from Earth. . . .

Like the recently published **Best Stories of H. G. Wells** (Ballantine S414K, 75¢), **The First Men in the Moon** is a key work by this acknowledged master, and an indispensable item in any science fiction collection.

Other Ballantine Science Fiction